SISTER MARYROSE

JOINS THE FBI

BY JANE CARACCI

Sister MaryRose joins the FBI
Copyright ©2013 by Jane Caracci
ISBN: 978-0-9885902-7-4
Library of Congress: 2013922576

La Maison Publishing, Inc.
www.lamaisonpublishing.com
ISBN: 978-0-9885902-7-4

This book is dedicated to my beloved husband, Joseph on our 60th year of marriage.

Many thanks to Jane Shannon and Diane DesRochers for their time, understanding, and most of all their love and friendship.

CHAPTER ONE

Tucker William Gillian, better known as Bill, is a senior partner of a large law firm in Washington, DC. He and his family lived in a suburb close to the city and decided it was time to leave all the congestion, crowds, and poor parking conditions in the city. His wife, Marianne, who teaches international law at Georgetown University, was also eager to move out of the city. Their three children were all for the move, as well as Mattie, the beloved housekeeper. They found a lovely area in Virginia, about twenty miles west of Arlington, called Plainview, which gave you the feeling of country living. The Gillians found a sprawling Cape Cod house built on three acres of land, which included a marvelous swimming pool and tennis courts. MaryRose, barely fourteen is the eldest and would go into high school ten days after they moved. Charles Tucker, known only as Chuck is eleven years old and the youngest, Charlyn is five. Mattie Harris refers to herself as the housekeeper, but the family considers her part of the family. Mattie came to live with the family shortly before MaryRose was born over fourteen years ago.

Marianne brought the two younger children to the parochial elementary school they would be attending which wasn't far from their new home. Chuck met his teacher and was delighted it was a man. Little Charlyn's kindergarten teacher wasn't available but she did see her classroom. On their way home, Chuck asked his Mom, "I didn't see any nuns at the school, I wonder where they were?"

"More than likely all the teachers will not be nuns, Chuck. There just aren't enough to go around," his Mother answered.

"They should call Auntie Marge and have her send some of the nuns from her convent"

"Those young women are at the Sisters of the Angels convent studying to become nuns."

"Well they should study on the job." Chuck answered.

In the meantime, Bill took MaryRose, (the family calls her Mair; rhymes with fair) to take a look at the high school. It wasn't a very big school, perhaps 1000 or so students. Mair was pleased to see some of the girls out on the soccer field. She loves the game and is a tremendous player. Bill introduced himself to the principal, Mr. Miller, and came away impressed. On the ride home, her father mentioned, "How about that soccer field Mair. Are you going to try out for the team?"

"Those girls look older than me, but hopefully they'll have a freshman team; I'll try out for sure."

It was evident at the dinner table that night everyone was pleased with their new surroundings and the schools. Little Charlyn chatted on and on about her classroom. When all the children were in their rooms for the night, Bill and Marianne sat in the den. "You know, honey, I think we hit the jackpot here."

"I think you're absolutely right," Marianne answered. "I'm so relieved the children are happy with the schools. The only one I was worried about was Chuck; both girls would be starting anew anyway."

"You think Mattie's content here? She's the one who's really making a big change. In the city she had a lot of friends, so her whole life wasn't just our kids."

"I think she'll be fine. Mattie seems to adjust to change easily. Heaven knows she's had many," Marianne replied

"You're probably right. You know, I should have asked Mair's principal, Mr. Miller where the closest church was." Bill mentioned.

"There's St. Joseph in Arlington. We could attend mass this Sunday and ask around if there's one closer."

"Good idea – and now my dear, I think I'll turn in. How about you?" She got up and said she was more than ready. They turned out the lights, checked the children, and snuggled together in bed.

Monday morning everyone was up bright and early. Mattie and Marianne were busy getting the children up, fed, and off to their first day of school. "Come on, Mom, we're going to be late," Chuck said, who was already in the driveway and Mair was not far behind. With all the children on their way to school, Mattie sat down at the kitchen table, took a deep breath, and relaxed with her second cup of coffee.

Mair's first week was more orientation and meeting her teachers as well as classmates. She found out athletics didn't start until the following week. Chuck not only liked having a man teacher, but he really liked Mr. Gibbs. This would be good news to his father. Chuck was a good student, but often needed a little push so liking his teacher was a plus. Little Charlyn wasn't sure about kindergarten and there were a few moments she thought she would go home, but by the end of the morning she forgot about leaving and joined in the games. That night at dinner, they all had news to share about school. Missy Charlyn talked the most.

9

The following week, MaryRose went to soccer tryouts. The girls were all freshman, which put them on an equal par; however, MaryRose had played soccer several years on municipal teams and played extremely well for her age. Of course, she hadn't played with any of these girls so her real expertise in the sport couldn't be evaluated with any accuracy. There are thirty-eight girls trying out and only eighteen would make the team. MaryRose was in the first group and she immediately stood out. She was put in the second and then the third group and it was obvious to the coach she is a fantastic player. Once the team was completed, they would play a nearby school team.

"I tell you, come take a look at this young gal. She is an outstanding player, and certainly would be an asset to your junior varsity team," the freshman coach told Mrs. Clark, the junior varsity coach. "It's your choice; all I asked you come see her."

"How tall is she? We have some tall gals on the varsity."

"She is five foot seven and still growing."

"Are the freshman still on the field?"

"Yes, come and take a look," MaryRose's coach said, and the coaches walked to the practice. Mrs. Clark sat on the bench as the freshman coach went out on the field. It wasn't long and Mrs. Clark was off the bench and on her feet amazed at what she saw.

The next week, MaryRose was playing with the junior gals and didn't disappoint anyone. When she got home, she couldn't wait to tell her parents. Actually, they knew. Mrs. Clark phoned her parents and wanted their approval of the switch. However, they didn't let on to Mair about the call.

Bill was told there was a little church, not from far from where they lived. So on Sunday morning the Gillians went to Saint Anne's. As they approach the church, Bill commented, "Yes sir, this is a small church, very small indeed."

"I like it. It might be small but it reminds me of the old country churches. It's beautiful," Marianne said. When the Gillians walked inside, they noticed it was indeed small and old, but it did have a certain charm. They also noticed the attendance was sparse. The priest was probably around forty years old, nice-looking, and more importantly gave a wonderful sermon. After mass, the priest stood outside to greet the parishioners. ,

"We are permanent residents of Plainview. We moved here about ten days ago." Bill told the priest.

"Excuse me, would you mind if I greet the few more parishioners? Stay right here, I do want to meet your family. Please." The Gillians moved aside while he greeted the remaining few. "Now tell me who's who?"

Bill introduced his family and when he got to Mattie said, "This is our permanent guest, Mattie. She's been with us for fifteen years. Now, Father, you have to introduce yourself."

"I'm sorry; my name is Father Paul Martin. I've been at Saint Anne's for three years. Are you the residents who have that beautiful Cape Cod home?" They chatted a few minutes and then Bill asked the priest if he would join them for brunch at the village Inn. "I'd love to but I have to clean up the sacristy – this was the last mass for today."

"No problem, we'll wait for you. We're in no rush."

"All right, I'll probably only be a half-hour behind you. Thank you so much. What a wonderful invitation."

"If you don't give us directions to the Inn, you'll be waiting for us," Bill laughed.

11

The Inn was an old Victorian home with a magnificent wraparound porch. The front porch had many white rockers and the side porches had table settings for outside eating. "Talk about charming," Marianne said. "This is lovely and I bet the food is great. Look at the mob here; I hope we can get a table."

Bill put his name on the list, "the hostess said it would be about twenty-five minutes." Fortunately, they were able to find four vacant rockers. Chuck went to the side lawn to play croquet and Charlyn wanted to watch. "Keep an eye on her," his father asked. MaryRose spotted a girl she just met in school, "Mom, can I go over to talk to Hillary, she's in my English class?"

"Sure, but keep an eye out for Father Paul." She talked to Hillary until her family's table was ready. Before Hillary entered the Inn, MaryRose asked, "When are the religious studies held at the church?"

"Write down your phone number and drop it off at our table when you guys come in." MaryRose nodded and went back to her family just in time to see Father Paul drive in.

They had a delightful time and Father Paul was a huge hit. Almost immediately after they were seated, Chuck wanted to know "Father, does the parish have a baseball team?"

"No Chuck, but suppose I asked from the altar who would be interested in joining your team. I just made you captain of the team. Is that okay?"

"Fantastic, Father. Do you think we'll get enough kids?"

"Well let's see. If not, maybe some of your classmates who live nearby would be interested. We'll get a team, Chuck, I'm sure." It was obvious the whole family liked their new parish priest, most of all Mattie. On the ride home, all she talked about what a caring and kind person he is. Several days later, Mattie made cookies for the family and some for Father Paul. She brought the cookies to the church that afternoon. He was doing some gardening in front of the church when Mattie arrived. "Father you're just the person I wanted to see. I made some cookies for the family and brought you a tin full."

"Mattie, Mattie you are an Angel from heaven. This is so kind of you." They chatted a few minutes before Mattie was on her way back home.

Every so often, Mattie would bring some food to the church knowing his facilities behind the altar couldn't be much. After doing this several times, one day Father was nowhere to be found, so Mattie thought she'd better put the food in the refrigerator behind the altar. She was shocked to see the rectory behind the altar, which consisted of a bed, small dresser, a makeshift shower, and small sink. No refrigerator, no stove, no closet – tears rolled down Mattie's cheeks. She thought *how could any man live like this, let alone the pastor of a church.* She put the food on the altar and left.

With dinner over, the Gillian children were busy with their homework. Mattie asked Bill and Marianne to come in the kitchen. She proceeded to tell them what she saw at church this afternoon, again with tears in her eyes. "It was a terrible sight. I just can't imagine how the good Father lives without the meager essentials needed."

"Mattie, I'm glad you told us, and I promise to do something about it starting tomorrow morning." Bill said, also finding it hard to believe.

On Monday, Bill left for his office earlier than usual, cleared off his docket for the day, took care of couple of things on his desk, and had his secretary call the office of Bishop McCann. When connected he convinced the Bishop's aid it was imperative he see the Bishop today, any time at his convenience.

"What is the purpose of this appointment?" The aide asked.

"Tell the Bishop it concerns the condition Father Paul Martin of Saint Anne's church is forced to live in." The aide asked Bill to wait a moment. He came back shortly and said, "Bishop McCann will see you at two forty-five this afternoon."

"Thank you, I will be there at two forty-five. May I ask whom I am talking to?"

"I am Father Thomas Kearney, the bishop's aide."

"Father Thomas, I look forward to meeting you and thank you for your help."

Indeed, Bill arrived at two fifteen and was ushered into an outer office. There he sat and two forty-five came and went, at three fifteen, Bill was admitted into the Bishop's office. After the formality due to the office of bishop, he was introduced to Bishop McCann. "From what I understand there is some problem at Saint Anne's"

"It is far more serious than a problem. It is a deplorable condition, which has to be addressed immediately. I think I should get to the point of my visit."

"Please do."

Bill gave him the entire description of how Father Paul was forced to live. "Just one moment Mr. Gillian, no one is forcing anything on Father Paul."

"I beg to differ. No one in your office or any other office had any idea what the condition of Saint Anne's church was at the time Father Paul was appointed to be the pastor." Bill suspected he might have gone too far, but felt strongly someone in the diocese failed. The Bishop said nothing for what seemed like many minutes.

Finally he spoke. "I've known Father Paul Martin for many years and he is without a doubt a fine and loyal priest to his vocation. I did assign Paul to Saint Anne's because according to our records, the church was losing its congregation and if anyone can bring in the faithful, it is Paul. You are absolutely right if what you told me is the way he's been living. It is deplorable and must be rectified immediately. Do you have solutions in mind Mr. Gillian?"

"Yes I do. I will buy a completely furnished trailer for Father to live in until a permanent rectory can be built."

"If you will supervise this project, I will see to it; the diocese will pay the costs."

"I will be only too happy to oversee the solving of the situation. I appreciate your kindness and pray our efforts will be fulfilled." Bill added.

Ten days later the trailer was delivered to Saint Anne's. Marianne and Mattie followed behind and directed as to where the trailer should be placed, per Bill's committee instructions. The women knew Father Paul would be teaching a religious class at this time. It was set in place just as the class was dismissed. The children came out first, and it took a few minutes before they discovered the trailer, but once they did, they swarmed all around. Father heard the commotion and came out.

"What in the world is a trailer doing here?" He was almost wordless. At that moment, Mattie and Marianne got out of the car and walked over to the priest.

"Father, the trailer is your new rectory," Marianne explained.

"Yes, Father Paul, and here are the keys; go inside and take a look." Mattie said, and was as excited as Father. The two women followed the priest inside; the man was speechless. He kept saying "for heaven's sake" or "good Lord" as he went from room to room. In the bedroom, kitchen and office the essentials were built in. It really was most attractive and both ladies had put in extra touches to make it cozy.

"I am at a loss for words. There aren't any words to tell you how grateful I am. I have a feeling your husband had a lot to do with this," Father said, with tear filled eyes, "Where is that man of yours anyway?" He asked.

"He had to be in court today but really wanted to be here. He just couldn't work it out and he didn't want to delay the trailer's arrival. I assure you though he'll be here before bed time tonight."

"He is quite a man. We all are blessed to have a man of laws."

"Yes, we are," Marianne agreed, "but right now I'd better get home and take care of his children."

"Talking about your children, I hear MaryRose made the junior soccer team. You'll have to let me know when her next game is scheduled; I'd love to see her." He took Marianne aside from the rest of the group and said, "Marianne, I see MaryRose quite often in church praying. I think there very well might be a vocation brewing within her. "

"Yes, you might be right. Both Bill and I thought so too, but feel at this point to let her grow up and have a better idea what God wants from her."

"Marianne, I couldn't have said it any better. She has so much to learn about life. Hopefully she will take the time to listen to God. Bless you – Go; I know you have to get home."

Marianne was right, Bill stopped at the new rectory before he came home for dinner. He knocked on the front door of the trailer and Father Paul opened the door and said, "How can I thank you, Bill."

"You can't, Father, because I'm not the one to thank. The Bishop is having the diocese pay for the trailer. "

"I know Bill, but I also know that if it wasn't for you, this trailer would never have been here. Bishop McCann called me late this afternoon and told me you came to see him and was very impressed. He also said you were not about to take no from him. I'm surprised he didn't have you removed from his office."

"There were a few moments I thought I would be dismissed promptly. Actually, he was very concerned when I told him the conditions your so-called rectory was in."

"By the way, how did you know? I never let anyone behind the altar. I guess I was embarrassed to say the least."

"Let's just say it was divine guidance, Paul and leave it at that. I had better run or I won't get any dinner." Bill left with Paul's blessings.

The following Sunday, Father Paul's sermon was about the gift from God, and he introduced the gift of man, "Bill Gillian, would you please come up here." Bill said no but finally accepted the invitation. I want you all to meet Saint Anne's financial advisor." The entire, congregation stood and clapped. Bill turned to Father and asked who said so, "The Bishop insisted," Father Paul said.

"I thank you, Father Paul, and I'd be honored to be Saint Anne's financial advisor. My first duty is to hope all parishioners will pitch in to make Saint Anne's what it should be – a parish that we all will be proud to belong. We need a keener interest and positive progress. Bless you all and now I have another Gillian to introduce you to – my son Chuck. Chuck come on up and tell them about the baseball team." Red-faced Chuck came up to the pulpit, took a deep breath, and began, "We need all of the young guys in this parish and beyond to form a baseball team. Father Paul said he would make a baseball diamond on the backfield. We could be great. We will be great. Thank you." He too got a standing ovation.

CHAPTER TWO

Bill and Marianne were up stairs getting ready for work when Bill said, "I haven't heard much talk from Mair. What's with her? Mair isn't one to put things off, certainly not as important as going to college. Isn't it time to be applying? Hasn't she said anything to you, Marianne?"

"I brought the subject up with her several times in the last couple weeks. All I get is she hasn't decided. She did say something about going to the library to look up the schools in the United States, but I never heard any more about it."

"Something's not right here," Bill remarked.

"I agree and I think we should get to the bottom of her lackluster attitude."

"Tonight after dinner – no wait a minute. Aren't I supposed to pick Mair up from soccer practice today?" Bill asked.

"Yes, that's right."

"How about we take her out to dinner? That way we can talk to her without family interruptions."

"Good idea, Bill. I can meet you at a restaurant. Let's say six fifteen. I have an early afternoon lecture, which works out fine. I'll be able to come home to get things organized. I'll let Mattie know before I leave for work."

MaryRose's soccer practice, although they seem to be all year round, will slow down somewhat with winter approaching. Now a junior and on the senior varsity soccer team, her spare time is really limited. Somehow, she seems to thrive on it though. Life at the Gillian household is in constant motion. Chuck is now a high school freshman and his love of baseball never waned, rather it intensified. He is now on the high school team, as well as Saint Anne's, which he's coaching and plays whenever the opportunity arises. Seven-year-old Charlyn, a second grader is on her school soccer team.

Bill had to cancel and called Marianne to pick up Mair at school instead, and then let him know where they plan to eat. He's sure he'll be able to meet them later.

"Where's Dad, I thought he was picking me up?" Mair asked her mother as she got into the car.

"I thought so too, but he called and is delayed, but hopes to meet us later."

"Meet us?"

"Well, we had planned to take you out to dinner and we're still doing so, but Dad will meet us later. First you have to tell me where you would like to have dinner so we can let Dad know."

"Am I missing or forgetting some occasion?"

"Dad said this morning we haven't had a one on one time with you in a long time, so he thought taking you out to dinner would be a good idea. You agree? Tell me where you would like to go?"

"I think its great Mom and the Outback suits me fine. I know you and Dad like going there as much as I do. Right?"

"Call your Dad's office and leave a message with his Secretary; we'll meet him at the Outback restaurant." They all arrived within five minutes of each other and their conversation began with Mair being on the senior varsity team.

Her Dad asked, "How is the team as a whole?"

"They work well together Dad and since I am almost five feet eight, I might be the youngest, but not the shortest. They really want to make state champs and with a lot of practice, I think we have an excellent chance."

"Sounds good, as long as all these practices won't distract you from your studies. This is a big year for you with applying to college. Actually, you'll get into in any college you want. However, you have to apply and get those applications in the mail soon."

"Dad, I'm glad you brought college up; some days I definitely want to go but on others I want to enter the convent."

"Where did that come from…I never heard you talk about having a vocation before?" her father asked a bit taken back.

"I just don't know what I want Dad. I've struggled over this decision for some time."

"It's a lifetime decision dear and a very serious one. Maybe Auntie Marge is the one you should talk to. She might be able to sort things out for you much better than either Dad or I can," her mother suggested.

"Mom, would you call her? I think you're right, she is the perfect person to advice me."

Marianne called her sister Marge the next morning and told her MaryRose had many decisions to make and she needed someone neutral to listen to.

"Give me a minute to check my schedule," her sister said. "How about Saturday morning around eleven o'clock? Is there a problem?" Marianne didn't go into any details; she was purposely vague. MaryRose was excited when her mother told her of the appointment.

Just before Mair was getting ready for bed she knocked on her mother's bedroom door, opened it to see her mother working at her desk. "Mom, I'm sorry to disturb you but I just was wondering if you told Auntie Marge why I needed to talk to her?"

"No, sweetheart, I didn't say a word only you wanted to talk with her. Mair, I didn't want to influence Marge in any way or tell her what I might think or what I might want for you. You want to hear what her thoughts are and not guided by my thoughts."

MaryRose was up at the crack of dawn Saturday morning; she could hardly contain herself she was so anxious to see Auntie Marge and her visit to the convent of The Sisters of Angels. As the Gillian family arose and went to the kitchen, they were surprised to see Mair already dressed and had her breakfast. "Going someplace?" Her brother asked.

"Mom and I are going shopping," she lied and looked at her mother who winked. Mair knew she got the message. She didn't want anyone to know they were going to the convent, which would perpetrate numerous questions. The duo left earlier than planned in order to calm Mair down. They got on the Parkway, which was the first time Mair drove on a highway. At first, her mother was a little nervous knowing Mair was running on adrenaline, but it wasn't long before she realized Mair was driving as well as anyone else. When they got a few miles from the convent, they stopped for a cup of tea. It was too early to see her aunt, Mother Mary Margaret.

Marianne drove off as soon as her daughter entered the convent's garden gate. She didn't want to go in with her, so this day would center all on MaryRose. She drove a few miles to the mall. Auntie Marge was sitting in the garden and as soon as she saw her niece, she walked to greet her.

"My beautiful MaryRose, I'm so glad to see you. I was thrilled when your Mom called, but I must admit a little curious."

"I can't tell you how happy I am to be here with you. I've told you many times God sent you to be my aunt." They both laughed and her aunt suggested they go to her office where they would have complete privacy with no interruptions.

Shortly after they were in the office, Auntie Marge asked, "What's up young lady; I hear your soccer team is up for the state championship."

"Yes, and I really think we have a good chance to win."

"While I was sitting in the garden waiting for you, it dawned on me this was the time of year to apply to college and I admit the time has flown by. It's hard to realize you'll soon be off to college; any idea where you might apply?"

"That's why I'm here, Auntie Marge. I'm not sure I want to go to college."

"What? I'm surprised. You know you could get in any college you applied to. I don't understand, what brought this about?"

"Auntie Marge, I think I might want to enter the convent instead." Tears streamed down MaryRose's cheeks. "I've been thinking about this for a long time. I want to serve God, but I'm not sure this is the right way. One day, I'm positive and then there are times when I'm not sure at all. I know Mom and Dad want me to go to college and I don't want to disappoint them either."

"Have they said you should go to college?"

"No, no. College hadn't even been discussed until the other night when Dad asked what college I was thinking of attending. He was concerned because it's getting late. I told them both I hadn't decided yet."

"Did you mention about going into the convent?"

"Briefly, and it was obvious Dad wasn't ecstatic although he didn't say much other than he was surprised. All Mom said it was an important decision and suggested I talk to you."

"Well then, let's talk about it. Your Mom is right about this decision being important and there are many things you need to discover about the convent and about yourself. One thing is for sure, if you have a true vocation, it will stay with you for life. MaryRose if we have twenty girls entering here at eighteen years old, after two years there might be seven, by the time for them to take their final vows, there probably will be only three. The ones who left after a year or two were like you very unsure of themselves or the decision they made. MaryRose you are trying to make grown-up decisions when you're not grown-up. Go to college, find out what's out there, date a nice boy, and have fun. After you've experienced these things, you'll know what you want. Most of all pray and ask God for his help. My dear, have I made any sense to you?"

"Oh yes. You've given me a lot to think about and you put things into perspective. Auntie Marge, how old were you when you entered?"

"I was thirty years old when I entered the convent and thirty-five when I took my final vows. Oh look, I see your Mom walking in the garden; shall we join her?" Auntie Marge asked as she came away from the window. MaryRose got up, hugged her aunt, and said, "Thank you so much, sometimes I think I just want to be like you, so thank you for being you."

"Honey, I would've loved to be like you. You are a very special person and have so much to offer this crazy world – go for it child."

23

Marianne noticed the change in her daughter as they drove home. Her whole self was alive and happy. She went on and on about her aunt and how she made everything feel worthwhile. "Mom, can I go to the library when we get home – I want to do some research on colleges." There was much talk at the dinner table that night as to what college MaryRose should attend. She read off the list of the colleges that she was interested in, "Boston University, Boston College, Harvard, Yale, MIT, Notre Dame, and Stanford University."

"Mair what's wrong with Penn State – that is where I want to go" Chuck declared.

Her father added, "Mair, that's a good list and apply to them all. There is no doubt in my mind you will be accepted to all, but time is running short and there is much for you to do. You'll have to get your transcripts, SAT scores, teachers' evaluations, recommendations, and above all your written essay, which really is the most valuable paper you'll send."

The next ten days Mair was busy collecting all the necessary documents needed and making photocopies. Her essay was finally written. Father Paul was coming to dinner with his recommendation to include in the mailings. With dinner finished, her Dad asked, "Mair I think you have everything needed so we can get them ready to mail, but first may I read your essay?"

While the dinner table was cleared, manila envelopes, addresses, piles of paper to include were place alongside each envelope. When Bill finished reading the essay he said, "Father Paul, you have to read this essay. Mair the essay alone would get you into any school in the world."

Mair went over to her Dad, kissed him on the forehead and said, "Thank you Dad, but aren't you maybe a little bit prejudiced"

"Not in the least. Truly, MaryRose, this essay is the best I've ever read. I can't say enough, you wrote a beautiful testament to life. As Father Paul, Mair and her mother checked each pile and put the papers in the envelopes, Bill was writing out the checks needed to accompany each application. The next morning they were mailed. Next came the waiting game, but Bill was positive his daughter would be accepted to all.

With the applications in the mail, and the holiday season behind her, Mair had to concentrate on winning the state championship in soccer. One of her teammates was in a car accident over the holidays and broke her leg in several places, so certainly won't be able to play again this season. She was a key player, which meant the team will have to practice some new plays. It is the end of February and the playoffs start the beginning of April, right before the senior prom. MaryRose wasn't too concerned about the prom since she didn't have a date anyway. She has a group of friends, both girls and boys and they hang out together, mostly at the Gillian home. They love their tennis tournaments and Mattie's goodies. As her Dad says, "They are a good group of kids."

"Mair, I'm a little concerned, you look so tired. Don't you think you're over doing it?" her Mom asked.

"Don't worry Mom, as long as I get enough sleep at night I'm fine. It won't be so hectic as soon as we figure out our plays without Sally. The very next morning, Mattie was concerned because Mair hadn't come down for breakfast and decided to go upstairs and see how come. When she opened Mair's bedroom door she was surprised to see her still in bed.

"MaryRose, you're late."

Rubbing her eyes Mair sat up and looked at the clock. "Oh my heavens, I'm really late." She jumped out of bed, ran into the bathroom, washed her face and hands, brushed her teeth, and combed her hair all in about five minutes. After getting on her soccer shirt and shorts, she ran downstairs. Mattie had already put juice and cereal out. Mair gulped it down and was out the door. As she was driving to school, she calculated how late she was; it was approximately fifteen minutes.

As soon as Mair arrived at school, she started to run to the soccer field. She thought she heard someone calling her name and turned and saw a boy but thought nothing of it. Mair continued to hurry. "Hey, MaryRose wait up." She slowed down, realized it was Tom Tyson, and couldn't imagine why he wanted to talk to her. "You are a hard gal to catch up with; I wanted to know if would go to the flick with me Saturday night."

"Oh, uh Tom, I'm so late now for practice. Call me tonight. Okay, my number is 321-6792."

MaryRose opened the gate to the field. She knew everyone on the team saw her talking to Tom. The entire school knows who he is since he's the Captain of the football team. She apologized for being late, but the girls said no problem as the coach was delayed also.

Sure enough, the phone rang as the grandfather clock chimed eight. Chuck answered and said, "Mair, some boy is on the phone for you!"

"Shush Chuck, why don't you act your age?" Tom and Mair talked for twenty minutes, Tom set the time he would pick her up, and yes, he knew where she lived. She sat on the floor by the phone and didn't understand the whole scenario. Why out of the blue would Tom want to go out with her when they never even talked or for that matter been in the same room. Now he knew her phone number and address. I just don't understand. At least my five foot eight will look short compared to his six foot plus, she thought.

The next day in school, MaryRose told her friend Hillary about Tom asking her out. "You have to be kidding. I didn't even know you knew him."

"I didn't – but he knew my phone number, my address and heaven knows what else he knows about me."

"Well, are you going out with him – and where?"

"He called last night, which really shocked me. He wants me go to the Saturday night movie."

"Are you going?" Hillary asked before MaryRose could say another word.

"He caught me off guard and I didn't know what to say, so I said yes."

"Do you know how lucky you are? Every girl in school would give anything to go out with Tom Tyson."

At seven forty-five, the Gillian's doorbell rang. Chuck practically ran to the door and as he opened it, "Hi, Tom it's nice to meet you. I'm MaryRose's brother, Chuck. Come on in, everyone is in the den – follow me." You could tell Chuck thought he was the man of the hour talking to the school's hero and star football player. As Chuck and Tom walked towards the den, Chuck yelled up the stairs to MaryRose, "Hey Mair, your date is here."

"I'll be down in a minute," Mair called down as Chuck and Tom entered the den. Tom introduced himself to Mr. and Mrs. Gillian, as Mair entered the den. The four of them chatted a few minutes and Tom said their goodbyes and were off. Tom was very polite and certainly a gentleman in the movie. He put one arm on the backrest of Mair's chair, which Mair didn't even know it was there. After the movie, they went to an all-night diner and talked mostly about their particular sport. Then he drove Mair home, walked her to the door, and said he would like to see her again soon.

Tom and Mair became an item. However, Tom became a fixture at the Gillian household and spent more time there than he probably did at his own home. He and Chuck played tennis and had tournaments going. Mair spent a great deal of her spare time at the soccer field. The state championship game wasn't far off. As much as Mair enjoyed seeing Tom, it really wasn't all that serious, as Tom would be leaving for college in a few months. Tom did ask Mair to the senior prom, which was a week after her junior prom. Mair then asked Tom to her prom. Both sets of parents were under the impression their children were quite serious about each other. "Time will only tell," was Mattie's thought.

CHAPTER THREE

"I can't believe it is junior prom night," Mattie said to those sitting at the breakfast table.

"Neither can I," Marianne sighed, "I'm not over the championship soccer game excitement yet. I hope the video Bill took shows the battle it took to win."

"I thought Father Paul would jump out of the stands." Chuck commented.

"Now we have to concentrate on tonight. Did Mair bring down her dress to be pressed?" Her mother asked. Mattie nodded as she had ironed it before people were strolling down to eat.

Just then the phone rang, "Hello...Let me check, I think I heard her upstairs...I'll get her. Mair, your boyfriend is on the phone again." Chuck yelled upstairs.

"Okay, I'll take it up here. Good morning, what time is it anyway Tom?" A sleepy voiced Mair asked. The two talked a few minutes then Mair came down to the kitchen. Tom had asked MaryRose to the prom more than a month ago which she refused. The reasoning was Tom being a senior had to go to his own prom. Two weeks later, however, Tom was persistent and finally got a yes answer when he said, "Mair, I'll ask you to the senior prom and you ask me to the junior prom. Now that's a deal you can't refuse, okay?" Mair laughed so hard she couldn't answer.

"Well, my lady friend?" He glared at her and she finally nodded her head yes.

Tom and MaryRose didn't date much, what with her practicing soccer and he playing basketball and then baseball. In his free time, he often went over to the Gillians to play tennis with Chuck or swim, whether Mair was home or not. If she was there, she often joined in. They had a nice relationship, although Tom would've liked it to be a bit more romantic. He didn't push it, knowing he would be leaving for college in the fall, and more importantly, they were such good friends, which meant a lot to both teenagers. He really didn't want to destroy that. Both proms were perfect. MaryRose look beautiful. Her long five foot eight frame was striking in a pale blue slinky gown with a slit to her knee. Tom was as handsome as she was beautiful. Father Paul came to get a glimpse of Mair ready for her first formal dance. At one point, he pulled Tom aside and Mair wondered what he said. When she asked Tom later all he would say, "He said, you look beautiful."

Two weeks later, Mair came down the staircase in a black and white creation. She looked stunning; although her dad thought it was too old for her, but then he's been saying the same thing since she was out of diapers. The night overshadowed her junior prom because this was an all-nighter, which didn't seem to bother Mr. Gillian. When Marianne questioned her husband why he wasn't bothered with her staying out all night with a young man, he said, "If there is anyone I trust more than MaryRose, they haven't been born yet."

The senior prom was more fun than MaryRose expected since she didn't know most of the kids. However, those kids knew her from her reputation on the soccer field. The couple danced a lot, and when the lights dimmed and Good Night Sweetheart played, Tom held her a bit closer and looked at her, "Mair, I have wanted to kiss you for a long time and I think now is the moment." Mair lifted her head and looked into his eyes and they kissed a long kiss. The lights came on brightly in the auditorium and the senior prom was over.

The next few days were filled with soccer practice readying for the playoffs at the end of the week. The team was well prepared and anxious for the game to begin. The entire school turned out for the big game. The Stadium was packed to capacity. Tom and Mair's brother, Chuck were right behind the girls dugout plus Father Paul and a good portion of Saint Anne's parishioners were at the game to cheer MaryRose on. It was a tight game and by the end of the last half, the score was 2 to 2. Our team noted the running clock only had six minutes left, and asked for time out. Every spectator was on their feet chanting, "MaryRose – MaryRose." The huddle broke apart, and the girls took their places. There wasn't a sound to be heard in the stadium. The play started and MaryRose started down the field slowly, her team protecting her against the opponents. Suddenly, she ran backwards for a moment or two, then quickly turned and charged down the field and scored. She and her team won the state championship to the roar of the crowd. The celebration went on into the night and ended up in Gillian's pool.

After Tom's graduation in May, life in the Gillian household calmed down a bit, although Chuck's Saint Anne's baseball team was in the County playoffs on the other side of Williams County. This caused a good deal of excitement, both in the church and the Gillian household. Since Chuck allowed every player on his team to play, some were good players and others not so good, but Chuck felt each boy should have a chance to play. The team lost the playoffs, but was written up in the local newspaper for their good sportsmanship...

Summer came and went and the Gillians once again, had each member picked an event they wanted the whole family to participate. They had a good summer and when Tom left college in mid-August, everyone missed him. MaryRose was surprised. She never thought of missing Tom, but then she didn't realize how much she liked him, or she never wanted to admit it. They never made love, but Tom's last night at home got pretty hot between them but stopped before it went too far. Tom did profess his love for Mair, but she did not. "There is no one in the world I care about more than you Tom, but I'm not sure what love is, and I don't want to say it, until I'm sure of myself and the word love." Tom replied, "I love you more than ever, and please, always be true to yourself."

In May of Mair's junior year the discussion of which college she wanted to attend was brought up again. She had done research in the library, asked some of the college advisors at school, and consulted Father Paul. She narrowed her choice down to two, Notre Dame and Boston College. At that time, MaryRose didn't know what major to choose; therefore, she decided on a liberal arts course. After lengthy discussions with her parents, she again went to Father Paul and told him she was leaning towards Notre Dame. Coincidentally he gave her a book on the same college, which he wanted her to read and come back then talk more.

MaryRose was so anxious to read the book. She read it over the weekend, which convinced her Notre Dame, was the college for her to attend. After the last mass on Sunday, Mair returned the book to Father Paul and said, "Father, I was so impressed by what I read. I'm sure I definitely want to attend Notre Dame. I really think it has everything I want to study.

"I rather thought you would find the information you needed to decide. To tell the truth, were it was my decision;

I too thought Notre Dame suited you to a tee. Have you told your decision to your dear Mom and Dad?"

"Yes, and I also called Auntie Marge and everyone was thrilled with the Notre Dame decision. My aunt thought I couldn't have chosen a better school, which could give me a fantastic all around education. Dad is ecstatic and I think Mom is just as enthusiastic as I. Father Paul, do you really think I'm headed in the right direction?"

"MaryRose I really don't know of a better direction for you take."

Her entire family agreed with the exception of Chuck; he thought Duke is the perfect college. "You come back to see me at Notre Dame and then you'll know why I've made the choice I did."

"But right now you're headed for your senior year in high school," Mattie pointed out.

"I've been doing a lot of thinking about what I want to do; one thing I'm pretty sure of, I will not join the new senior varsity soccer team."

"How come?"

"I've been playing soccer since I was seven years old, and you know I love the sport, but I think this year I would rather coach the team."

"Why's that?"

"I guess it's researching and figuring out the girls, their abilities and what drives them, how ambitious their thinking and how they work together. More important is how they get along with each other."

"Sounds good, Mair, but is the position open? You had some great coaches, while you played," her father remarked.

"We sure did, but I heard Mrs. Stern is retiring, plus all I would be is an assistant coach. Therefore I won't be taking anyone's place."

MaryRose's senior year seemed to fly by. Tom Tyson did come home for Christmas holidays and he most likely spent more time at the Gillians than in his own home. Mair was glad to see him and the spark was still there between them. He did say he wouldn't be home for spring break since he made the college baseball team. However, he did want to know Mair's graduation date and the senior prom.

"Well, how will you be able to make the prom or graduation?"

"Mair, I asked you to mine, and naturally I thought you'd asked me to yours."

"Oh, is that the plan?"

"Absolutely."

"If that's the case, I guess we better wait and see what the dates are for me and your baseball game dates."

Actually, their schedules never coincided for either event. MaryRose went to the senior prom with a classmate who was also a friend at Saint Anne's religion classes – Ted Sorenson

Mair left for Indiana to go to orientation in early August. She had made contact earlier in the summer with her college roommate, Jenna Walsh. They exchanged pictures and emails and both felt they made a good combination.

Therefore, a new beginning started for MaryRose. So many things changed in her life and she realized it is true what Auntie Marge said about how you're not only growing up, but so is your thinking. Mair still thought and wondered about her life in the convent and giving her life to God, but she knew she would have to first know and learn about so many things.

Mair's relationship with Tom grew less and less as each year passed. They both knew time apart would minimize their feelings for each other. She also realized she never knew if her feelings for Tom were love or just an infatuation. Occasionally she thought about Tom and she didn't like thinking of him seriously dating someone else but those thoughts made her laugh. How little I know about love and life; I do have a lot to learn Auntie Marge. A smile crossed her face and she was deep in her thoughts.

Her parents drove Mair to Notre Dame and they were as excited for their daughter as she was. They were directed to her dorm room, where Mair was glad to see Jenna already there. They hugged each other like they were old friends. Mair introduced Jenna to her parents, who also gave the girl a big hug. "I'm so happy to finally meet you face-to-face, although I feel like I know you well from all our correspondence," a smiling Mair said.

"Me too, I thought you'd never arrive; I flew in last night and stayed at the guesthouse."

"I understand there is a lunch served for all new students and parents. How about we all go have something to eat?" Mair's father declared nodding his head.

"Good idea Bill and then we can get going and let these ladies get settled," his wife agreed. Young ND men were at their disposal to bring belongings from the parent's car to the rooms, which made life a lot easier for Dads.

It wasn't long before Jenna and Mair had gotten their suitcases, and boxes unpacked and put their belongings away. They arranged the furniture to suit their fancy. The room had a bay window, so they shared the space by placing their desks back to back in the bay. All in all, when finished, they agreed that they had great living quarters. The girls signed in and the rest of the afternoon, they explored their building as well as the campus. Freshman orientation was the next morning. College life was about to begin.

The next four years in MaryRose's life were amazing. She couldn't put in words how much she learned and the knowledge she gained, plus how she grew within herself. She was a liberal arts major and took many side electives. Mair became aware of her love in researching and investigating. She didn't participate in many athletics, although she was on the winning tennis team. She also was a reporter on the school paper, becoming the editor before getting her degree.

She became involved with the Basilica of the Sacred Heart, which was on campus along with the religious order, Holy Cross. She had no knowledge of the order or about Holy Cross priests and brothers. She discovered Notre Dame was founded by one Holy Cross priest and six brothers who came from France. She found counsel in one particular priest, Father Pierre. If she chooses to go to Mass during the week, the college has dorm masses at 9 PM.

MaryRose even had a little time for some social life. Jenna became involved with Stan, a neat guy, but she and Mair remained close friends throughout college. Jenna also carried a heavy schedule, but on the weekends, Stan was in the picture. Frequently Stan asked Mair to join them, which she did sometimes, but more often was too busy. One Friday afternoon, he and the girls were having lunch together, when Stan asked, "Mair have you met the new guy on campus, Rusty Cooper?"

"No, but I've heard a lot of talk about him. Why? Do you know him?"

"Yeah, he rooms next door to me. He's a neat guy and stands out with his English accent."

"He's from England?" asked Jenna.

"Yes, yes I have seen him," Mair broke in. "It seems every girl on campus wants a date with him."

Stan started laughing and in between his laugh said, "I'm sorry, Mair, but I have to say every guy on campus wants a date with you."

"Oh come on Stan; no way is that true."

"Mair, I'm not kidding, as a matter of fact, Rusty said so at a wrestling practice yesterday."

"I doubt so."

The next day as Mair was walking to her next class with Jenna. Suddenly, Stan and Rusty were standing right in front of them. Stan immediately introduced Rusty to Mair, "Mair, this is Rusty Cooper – Rusty meet Mair."

Mair actually blushed and this started what would become a lifetime friendship, although there were times when the friendship leaned towards romance. Once Rusty found out the name Mair stood for MaryRose, Rusty called her M-rose. The couples became a foursome around campus and needless to say, Mair was the envy of many girls. However, both Rusty and Mair are well aware come graduation, Rusty would leave for England.

During Mair's summer vacation, she told her Dad she was thinking about going to law school, which pleased her Dad beyond words thinking she would eventually come into his law firm. Back to reality, he said her selection was perfect and asked, "Are you thinking of Notre Dame's law school?"

"It's high on my priority list, although I'm looking into several others." The father-daughter conversation was cut short by Mattie. "Mair, you have a visitor at the front door."

"Who?"

Mattie just smiled as Mair headed for the front door. "Since when, Tom, do you come to the front door instead, of coming through the kitchen to get a cookie or two from Mattie?"

"I wanted to make sure I was welcomed."

"Come off of it Tom. We better go into the kitchen or Mattie will be insulted." They both sat at the kitchen table with Mattie and ate some of her special cookies. After a while, Mattie excused herself and Mair and Tom remained and once they relaxed, talked about each of their college activities, studies, and future plans.

After an hour or so Mair told Tom, she had an appointment with Father Paul and added, "Tom, it is good to see you. I hope we'll get the opportunity again." Mair walked him out to the driveway and his car. Tom opened his door and turned towards Mair and he put his arm around her and bent to kiss her "Tom, those days are over. You know it as well as I, but I hope we will always be good friends and always remember our good times growing up."

"Mair, you still have the knack of saying the right things at the right time. You're right and I will always hold you in my heart as someone very special." Mair looked up, kissed him on the cheek, and then watched him drive away with tears in her eyes.

CHAPTER FOUR

The first thing Mair did when she returned to school was make an appointment with the pre-law advisor, Mr. Burkhardt. The appointment was set for the following Thursday. He put Mair at ease the moment she walked into his office. He was informative and told her how important it is to prepare now to succeed in law school. She also would need an excellent GPA and a high scoring LSAT. He continued by saying, "Right now, Miss Gillian, choose your electives here at Notre Dame which will prepare you to write well, think logically and analytically."

"Mr. Burkhardt, when do we take the LSAT?" Mair asked.

"The June following your junior year. The LSAT is a half day standardized test. Your score will be mailed to you in July, giving you ample time to begin the process of selecting a law school."

"Thank you so much, Mr. Burkhardt, you have been very helpful. I appreciate your time and advice." Then he handed her a list of how to prepare for the LSAT and before Mair left he said,

"Miss Gillian, this isn't the first time, and no doubt the last time, I have heard your name and your exceptional scholastic abilities. If you really want law school, I suggest you continue what you are doing and work hard. If I can be of any further help, the door is open."

MaryRose was glad to be home on her Christmas break. The first part of her junior year at ND was hectic, mostly making sure she was ready for the LSAT test. For once in her life, she was glad to be away from the books. However, she had much to decide and a great deal to talk over with her Dad about school.

Mair was anxious to see her brother, Chuck. He did go to Duke and is now a sophomore. Little Charlyn, who wasn't so little at five foot-five inches, was about to graduate and start high school in the fall. It will be good to have the family all together. *I can't wait*, Mair thought. When everyone was finally home, Mair made a point to go into Chuck's room late at night, just to chat and catch up on how he was hoping to make his life worthwhile. She did the same with Charlyn, who was picture-perfect and growing up to be a lovely gal.

Christmas dinner was planned for late in the afternoon so Father Paul was able to join them. He got Mair aside and asked her to come over to the rectory to have a chat, which she did the following evening. "I hear you're planning law school."

"Yes, Father Paul, I really got caught up in research and investigating at Notre Dame, and I spoke to Mr. Burkhardt a law advisor and an amazing person. He convinced me it would be a good career choice."

"I'm sure he's right; I hadn't realized your interest in law. I don't know why I didn't with both your Mom and Dad lawyers. Now that I think about it – it certainly seems logical. Tell me, do you have a love interest in college?"

"I date a very nice young man, Rusty Cooper, a boy from England. We're not all that serious, but we do have great times together. He has an amazing personality. Just a neat guy; I think you'd like him."

"Yes, I'm sure I would," Father agreed. MaryRose couldn't put her finger on it, but got the feeling what they were discussing wasn't at all what Father Paul wanted to discuss.

"Father, what is it you want to talk about? I have the feeling you're beating around the bush."

"You are perceptive. No doubt, I should've known better. Yes Mair, I was wondering if your desire and interest in the vocation you thought you might have is still sitting in the back of your mind. Before you answer, I have to apologize for being such a klutz."

MaryRose smiled and said, "Father, there is a Holy Cross priest, Father Pierre, at the Basilica at Notre Dame who has been a tremendous help to me. We have spent many hours talking about the possibility of my having a deep and sincere vocation."

"What is his opinion?"

"Oh, the vocation is still there, but as Father Pierre pointed out there are many facets to a vocation and he has helped me research within myself how to follow what God wants of me. There are still days I long to enter the convent, and too, many days I feel I am doing what God wants now. So you see Father Paul, I guess as Auntie Marge said, I'm growing and learning and God will let me know in time what's next for me."

The two friends talked for several hours and it became obvious Father Paul didn't feel Mair was ready to enter a convent and thought she might never be. He felt she has so much energy, which makes her continually seek more challenges. To put the conversation on a lighter level, he questioned, "Tell me about this English fellow; is his name Russell?"

MaryRose smiled and was glad for the relief. "You know Father, I don't know him other than Rusty; I'll have to ask him." Father Paul smiled, knowing full well Mair knew exactly why the change in conversation.

Once back at Notre Dame, Mair immediately got back to accomplishing what was left on her law advisor's LSAT list. The remainder of her junior year seemed to fly by, and many of the students were getting ready to head home, including Rusty, Jenna, and Stan. Prior summer breaks, Rusty previously stayed in Indiana, but said there was a matter he had to attend to this summer in England. Jenna was going to her hometown and Stan is going to his home, but only for a short time before heading back to see Jenna.

When test day arrived Mair was prepared for the LSAT, although a little nervous. Mr. Burkhardt's list was purposely extensive and somewhat in excess of what the test required. Mair took the allotted amount of time before she handed her completed test to the monitor. She had her luggage packed and immediately headed home to Virginia. Mattie was worried because Mair spent the first two days at home, mostly in bed. Her Mom assured Mattie it was a normal reaction after the strain she had been under.

"Good morning MaryRose – and you're dressed, which I hope means you'll not retreat to your bed," Mattie said as she gave Mair a hug.

"You know Mattie - I don't think I've ever been so tired."

"Well, you're right where you belong, so sit back, and relax. While you are sitting let me get the mail that arrived for you."

One letter was from the Tyson family inviting her to Tom's after graduation party at their home. She passed it for Mattie to see, but Mattie said, "Yes, I've seen this. Chuck received the same invitation."

"That's good, and then I'll have someone to go with," Mair said as she was opening the envelope from

England. As she opened it, she walked into the sunroom and began to read the contents. She sat on the lounge and reread the letter from Rusty. It was full of his wonderful sense of humor and brought broad smiles to Mair's face. He is so full of fun, this guy…I really do miss him. I surprise myself. Why does reading his letter show me I miss him? Why don't I allow myself to admit it? Maybe I should see a psychologist. These "whys" have plagued me often, she thought. After reading Rusty's letter, she went back in the kitchen and Mattie handed her two other envelopes. One was from Jenna and the other from her law advisor, Mr. Burkhardt, which she ripped open immediately. All he said he was glad to have worked with her and was sure the results would be favorable. In Jenna's letter, she told Mair how much she missed her and to keep in touch over the summer. She also asked how the LSAT test was.

"Mattie, is Chuck home?" Mair asked.

"I'm not sure, he might be on the tennis court or over at Saint Anne's."

"When you see him, please tell him I want to talk to him. I'll be in Dad's study writing some letters." Mair did write a note to Rusty and was going to write Jenna, but decided to call her, which turned out to be an hour-long conversation.

Mair and Chuck went to the party at the Tyson's and it was good to see Tom. They talked to him briefly, then cut out and went to Saint Anne's to see Father Paul.

As usual, each family member was making a list of what event they wanted to do with the family over the summer. Mair was very hesitant to do anything the first couple of weeks of July, since she was anxious to receive her LSAT score. Chuck also had baseball tryouts for the kids at Saint Anne's. Therefore, the family decided, due to the conflicts, they would take a four-day cruise the first of August. Finally, the awaited letter arrived with Mair's test results and as anticipated, she passed with more than favorable scores. She was excited but now she must decide where to attend law school. When her parents arrived home from work, the three sat together out on the sun porch. Mattie decided to take Charlyn to the movies and Chuck went out with one of his college buddies making it possible for Mair and her parents to have complete quiet privacy. They were thrilled with Mair's news.

"I'm sure Mair, you have thought where you might like to attend law school, or are you going to stay at Notre Dame?" Her father asked.

"I have thought about it a great deal, and also consulted Notre Dame's law advisor, along with numerous others."

"Did any decision come out of those discussions?"

"No positive decision, but I have narrowed the field down to two, both of which I want your input."

"Let's hear them," her mother anxiously said.

"One is Notre Dame, which has a great law school and I know a couple of the professors who I like a lot. The second one and I'm not putting either in order of preference... Number two is both of yours alma mater, Harvard." The three talked making a point to separate the schools according to their different curriculum and status.

During their long talk her Dad said, "Mair, both your mother and I received a fantastic law education at Harvard Law school. No matter which school, there are difficult courses to learn. This doesn't bother me as far as you are concerned. I feel Notre Dame is certainly a superior school. What I am saying darling is, I'm putting the ball in your park; it is your decision and yours alone."

"I'm delighted these are your thoughts, because I want to follow the tradition you both have set for me. I will apply to Harvard."

With MaryRose's decision to go to Harvard Law School made, she was ready for the some fun the rest of the summer. The family's four-day cruise is what Mair needed and no doubt, the entire family needed it too. Mair tried to spend as much time with Charlyn, as possible. Charlyn came to Mair's cabin the first night out to sea and was crying. "Charlyn, what's the matter?" Mair asked as she put her arm around her sister.

"I just feel sad. Pretty soon you'll be gone off to school again, and so will Chuck and I'll be all alone."

"Sweetie, we'll have to make a point to do things together more often before I go back to school but you're never alone. Just think. You, Mom, Dad, and Mattie will be the fearsome-foursome. Plus, the fact, every time I turned around this summer another one of your friends was at the house. Remember next year you'll be in high school, and then poor Mattie and Mom and Dad will be alone." which brought a big smile to Charlyn's face and she sat on the bed with Mair and talked and talked to almost midnight when Charlyn drifted off to sleep. Mair took off her shoes covered her up and tiptoed to the door. She went to her parent's suite where Charlyn had the adjoining room and told her mother that Charlyn was going to sleep with her.

The Gillians were home from their cruise only a few hours when the doorbell rang, Mattie alone in the house, opened the door to a young man who she never had laid eyes on before and said, "May I help you?"

"Yes, ah yes. Is MaryRose home – here, I mean," the lads tumbled his words in his English accent.

"Come in, you must be Mair's friend she met at Notre Dame."

"Yes indeed. I hope I'm not interrupting anything coming unannounced like this."

"Is MaryRose expecting you?" Mattie questioned.

"No, no. I know it's rude of me, but I thought I would surprise her."

"Okay. I think she's out at the pool. I was going to call out there. Instead, why don't you walk out to the pool and surprise her," Mattie said as she led him to the sunroom door. "The pool is just beyond those shrubs...follow this path and you'll see it." The young man thanked Mattie and headed for the pool, perhaps a bit nervous, Mattie thought.

Rusty spotted Mair sitting on a lounge chair reading. He silently walked up behind the chair and said, "How is my M-rose today"? Mair slowly put down her book like she was hearing things. Rusty then stood in front of her, "M-rose I'm so glad to see you. I have missed you." Mair got off the lounge, stood for a moment and then fell right into Rusty's waiting arms.

Mair still wasn't over the shock of seeing Rusty when the entire family, including Rusty was at the dinner table. Everyone was taken with the young man's English accent. It was also obvious, everyone was taken with Rusty himself. Mair sat back in her chair while dessert was served and looked over her family and their reaction to Rusty. He really is charming, she thought.

They were due back at Notre Dame in three weeks' time and Bill Gillian suggested Rusty stay in the guest rooms above the garage. Bill actually had a hard time convincing the young man to stay. He finally condescended but you could tell he felt awkward.

Rusty and M-rose had a marvelous three weeks. Mair enjoyed being able to show Rusty the capital with all the historical monuments and Arlington Cemetery. They drove down to Norfolk, swam in the ocean, and in the evenings at home took long walks. It was obvious to all they were more than just friends. On one such walk, they sat on the side of the hill after walking several miles from the house. The full moon shined brightly as M- rose laid back in the thick grass. Rusty looked down at her and smiled. Eventually his lips touched hers and he pulled her close to his body. "M-rose I am in love with you and I want you to be mine – I want to marry you so we'll never be apart again." He whispered in her ear.

"You are my love and if we could go on like you said, I'd marry you tonight." she sighed.

"M-rose we could go on like this, right after graduation. I know you are going to law school and I'd be able to get a job for sure, and help you in any way you needed."

"Hold me Rusty, hold me tight. I never felt this way before. I want to treasure the moment." The two lovers made passionate love that night in the moonlight. Rusty opened her blouse and kissed her full breast. "I want to lay naked with you." Rusty whispered as they took off their clothes. They rolled together and made love as the thick grass rubbed against their bodies.

They dressed and walked hand-in-hand in silence back to her house. Finally, Rusty's M-rose said, "I never told anyone I loved them, partly because I didn't know what physical love was. I only knew the love I felt in my heart."

"Do you love me in your heart, M-rose?"

"Yes I think I do. Give me time Rusty to find myself."

"You can have all the time you need. Just remember I'm here for you always."

They arrived at the sun porch door, kissed and said good night. She went upstairs, he went to his loft above the garage, and they both were smiling.

CHAPTER FIVE

As the Gillians drove along the Parkway towards Indianapolis, Mair's mother noted her daughter's thoughts were somewhere else. Ever since Rusty left a few days ago to fly back to Notre Dame, Mair seemed deep in thought and far away. Both her parents knew that Rusty and Mair's friendship went to another level, but nothing was said by anyone. "I think our daughter is falling in love," Bill noted soon after the young man left.

"It could be," Marianne agreed. "I would think Mair would be excited, happy, and all aglow, but she's quiet and into herself these last couple of days."

As they neared the campus, Bill looked in the rearview mirror and saw Mair asleep with Charlyn's sleepy head on her big sister's shoulder. "Girls, wake up were here…wake up." Bill called.

"Oh, my heavens we're here already?" a sleepy voiced Mair said as she looked out the window at what was now familiar territory.

"Yup, are you and Jenna in the same dorm?"

"That's a good question Dad; let me get out the letter. It'll have all the info." Mair opened her purse and read the ND mail she received. "Well, here it is," she said and read on. "Okay, no. We're in what they call the send-off building," she laughed. "It's just around the corner. Yes, right there, see Jenna and…Rusty sitting on the curb." Mair's heart skipped a beat.

"Good, he can help me carry this load to your room." her father happily said.

Rusty was a big help and it wasn't long before everything was in place, and then Rusty walked directly to M-rose; took her hand and asked to be excused.

He led Mair out the door and down to a sitting room. He closed the door behind them, took M-rose in his arms, and kissed her. "M-rose I have to leave in a few minutes, but I had to wait to see you first."

"What are you talking about? Where are you going?"

"A telegram was waiting for me when I arrived here from your home."

"What telegram? What did it say? Tell me Rusty."

"M-rose my father died, I guess it's a week ago now and of course my Mom didn't know I took a shortcut to your house before getting to ND. Here I was falling in love with my special M-rose and they couldn't find me. There is much to talk about, but I do have to leave now…I have about thirty minutes to catch my plane to England. As soon as I get there, I'll call you. In the meantime, keep me in your heart." Rusty pulled her near, kissed her long, hard, turned, and went out the door. Mair sat down in the nearest chair, trying to comprehend what she just heard. It was fifteen minutes or so before she went to her parents and Jenna.

Mair never saw Rusty at Notre Dame again. At first, he wrote frequently from England but the letters lessened as Mair's senior year passed. Rusty was the oldest son of five in the Cooper household. His family came to depend upon him for many things, most of all financial support, so he went to work as an apprentice with a local newspaper.

Mair went headfirst into her studies. She took some pre-law courses mainly to discover what kind of law would be her forte. During the Christmas break, she went home with Jenna to Arkansas as she and Stan were married Christmas Eve with Mair the maid of honor. After all the wedding festivities, Mair flew to Virginia and spent time with her family before going back to school. It was during then she made a point to see Auntie Marge.

"You look marvelous MaryRose it's been too long since I've seen you, but I think I've kept up to date through conversations with your Mom." the Mother Superior smiled so happy talking and seeing her niece. "You are all grown up, aren't you, my dear?"

"It is hard to believe I've reached the ripe old age of twenty-one, plus I am of legal age now." MaryRose laughed. "Seriously, it's good to see you and you're right, it's been too long. I needed your advice many times."

"Oh, my dear, from what I hear you're doing just fine on your own."

"Remember Auntie Marge, you get your information from Mom and Dad."

"What is that supposed to mean?" The nun asked.

"I guess Mom doesn't know everything about me, at least my private thoughts and desires."

"You are probably right, but never sell your parents short."

"Auntie Marge, it's the time in my life they shouldn't want to know what's in my head and heart."

"Do you want to share those issues with me?"

"Auntie Marge, up until before I went back to college this past fall, I had everything I wanted to accomplish in my head, exactly what was right for me, and I was certain what God wanted from me. I am sure Mom told you about the English boy I met at ND, Rusty Cooper." Her aunt nodded. "He was so much fun to be with whether we were alone or with a group…For that matter we were seldom alone. His sense of humor is fantastic…just a neat person. He arrived in Virginia, three weeks before we were to return to ND, to surprise me. Those three weeks I think where the happiest of my life. A couple of nights before he left he told me he loved me and wanted us to marry. "Mair hesitated for a full moment or two, and finally continued, "Auntie Marge we made love – we had intercourse." By this time, tears were flowing down her cheeks. Her aunt smiled and kept her composure as if lovemaking is perfectly all right.

Her aunt simply asked, "Do you love this young man?"

Through tears and sobs she cried, "I don't know, although I do miss him, and at times I long to see him. But then, I'm not sure I even know what love is, or how you should feel inside. The sad part is I may never see Rusty again. His father died while he was visiting us in Virginia and Rusty had to return to England before senior year even started."

"Will he be returning to Notre Dame to finish this year?"

"I doubt it; he is the oldest of two brothers and two sisters, so he had to find work to help support his mother and siblings. He wrote practically every day until he got a job and now I hear every once in a while. I write quite often," she hesitated for a minute or two before she continued, "but lately I find little to say knowing graduation is just a few months away; he would love to be here too. He really wanted a degree from Notre Dame."

Neither woman said anything for a few minutes, then MaryRose blurted out, I know Auntie Marge, I betrayed you and all you stand for...and God."

"No, my dear, if there is any betrayal it is to yourself and it really isn't betrayal as much as guilt. You allowed your emotions to take control." Mother Superior and MaryRose talked for several hours about what God expects from us and reminded her, "We have a forgiving God,

MaryRose. Then the two women talked at length of her acceptance into Harvard and the possibilities there after.

MaryRose hugged her aunt and said, "How can I ever thank you for putting me back on the right track. I learn many life experiences from you. Now I must go, but I thank you and thank God for you."

The nun watched her niece walk to her car and smiled. She thought life isn't always the way we'd like. We face many curves in the road of life, but one must be strong and have faith. "God bless you," she said and waved as her niece drove away.

MaryRose returned to Notre Dame after the holidays, as did Mr. and Mrs. Stan Strong. However, Jenna has a steady roommate now so Mair went to registration and found there was a Chinese girl in need of a roommate. She met Myling who spoke English. As tall, as MaryRose is Myling was only five feet maybe even shorter. At first, she was very quiet and Mair thought shy. Mair, with her investigating powers went to the library and found a lot of helpful material on the customs where Myling lived in China. She also was a great help showing Myling the customs of Notre Dame.

By the end of January Myling was comfortable at ND, which her perfect English helped. The roommates found they had many interests in common. Myling had gotten her college degree in China, but is taking pre-law courses at ND. She wanted to familiarize herself in American college life before attending Harvard.

Classes were finished with only two weeks until graduation and Mair decided not to go home; rather she stayed with Jenna and Stan. Myling left for China to spend the summer with her family, and in the fall, she would go directly to Harvard. Mair and Jenna's genuine friendship made it difficult, knowing they would have separate lives after graduation, but promised to keep in touch. Mair is staying with the Strong's for the two weeks made it all the more special.

Bill Gillian made reservations for his family at the Inn, located on Notre Dame's campus almost a year prior to graduation. The entire family left Virginia for Indiana; Mair's Mother and Father, Chuck, Charlyn and Mattie. Bill rented a small U-Haul-It to take care of Mair's belongings in order to keep the car free and the passages comfortable. Six foot plus Chuck took the space of two. Most of the trip he sat up front with his Dad leaving the three females delegated to the back.

Mair and Jenna were at the designated spot on campus to meet the arriving Gillian family. Mair was anxious to see them, and was actually pacing while waiting. Finally, she spotted the car, which wasn't hard as her Dad started honking his horn the moment he saw her a block away. After hugs and kisses they all piled back into the car, Mair directed her Dad to the Inn, where her family would be staying.

"Dad, how come the U-Haul?"

"Well, I thought it would be enough space for your long legged brother," her father joked.

"It probably is a good idea; I have a bunch of stuff at Jenna's house to bring home. Leave it to you Dad, always thinking ahead of everyone else." Mair admitted.

The family had a quick supper in one of the school's cafeterias before retiring for the night. It had been a long trip and everyone was tired, except Chuck. He went back with Jenna and Mair to pick up most of Mair's belongings left at the Strong's house. Commencement weekend starts the next day, so they didn't stay very long, but saying goodbye to Jenna and Stan was difficult. They had been good friends during their entire four years at Notre Dame.

On a bright sunny Saturday morning, the Gillian family had a late breakfast at the Inn, and afterwards Mair showed the family around campus, including her old room. Mair had to leave them to find her place in the procession. The graduates filed into the Mass according to their specific degree. It was a beautiful Mass with an inspiring homily given by the University president. This was followed by the commencement dinner at each of the two large Notre Dame dining rooms.

The following day, the Commencement Ceremony was at Notre Dame Stadium. All the different degree students filed in procession with their tassels designating the different colleges. The day was cool with variable clouds, but all were thankful for no rain; rain or shine, the ceremony would take place. Each college was recognized with cheers, followed by degrees handed out. Of course, families of each graduate stood up in the Stadium and cheered. It was sundown before the ceremony concluded and dark before everyone found their car and departed the Stadium grounds. It was late that night before graduates got to bed, for sure.

The next morning everyone slept later than usual, with the exception of Mattie, who was so used to early rising to get breakfast and the family on their way. It is difficult for her to sleep in. Mattie didn't even hear Mair come in. When she finally got up Mair didn't know what time she arrived at the Inn either. There were many street parties, departure parties and goodbye parties, which took place most of the night.

"What time did you finally get here last night?" questioned Chuck. He was with Mair a good deal of the time until he got lost and had to find his way back to the Inn himself.

"Hey, I was looking for you…All of a sudden you up and disappeared." Mair said

"Cripes Mair, there were so many people and I met up with a guy whose brother I knew at Duke. When I turned around you were nowhere in sight."

"When I got in I was so glad to find you in bed. I had visions of roaming the streets looking for you," Mair said.

"Now everyone is awake and accounted for…I am starved, so let's go to the dining room and hope they are still serving breakfast," Bill Gillian said as he ushered all out the door.

With everyone fed, packed, and settled in the car, the Gillians drove to Jenna and Stan's house to pick up a few of Mair's belongings she left.

"I have to tell you, I'm glad we have the U-Haul," Bill commented, as the last piece filled the storage unit. Chuck and Stan did most of the lugging and packing the unit, which Mair appreciated. There were several minutes…actually another half hour, while Jenna and Mair said a final sad farewell. Finally, the Gillians were on the road home to Virginia.

'It's hard to believe someplace so familiar for four years; I'll probably not see again…" Mair didn't finish because her eyes were filled with tears. She really enjoyed her years at Notre Dame and was sorry to leave.

Bill made the trip in one day, one long day. They pulled into their driveway at midnight and left the unpacking until morning. Everyone was ready for bed. Chuck helped Charlyn upstairs and she laid her sleepyhead on her pillow. He yelled downstairs, "Good night."

Both Marianne and Bill had to go to work the next morning and found Mattie in the kitchen making breakfast. No one woke up Charlyn, even though she would miss school. Chuck had a ballgame at the church, but it wasn't until four in the afternoon so he was left alone sleeping, as was MaryRose.

Mair strolled into the kitchen around ten in the morning and Mattie was ready with her favorite omelet. "Oh, it is good to be home," she said while stretching.

"I can't tell you how empty the house seems without you and Chuck. Here sit down and enjoy," Mattie put the omelet in front of her and Mair took in its aroma and chowed down.

"By the way Mair, there are several letters I put aside for you and I picked up these in today's mail also addressed to you." Mair thumbed the envelopes and they all were postmarked England.

"Mattie, I'll take my coffee out on the sun porch. The breakfast was wonderful, as usual," Mair said as she picked up her letters and headed for the porch. She got comfortable and opened the letters, according to the postmark dates. Rusty had much to write about; he got a better job paying twice as much, is going to college at night to get his degree, his Mom and siblings were all well, and his heart aches to be with Mair. He expressed his love many times over, as well as how much he missed her. She no sooner finished his last letter, and the doorbell rang. Mattie came out to the sun porch with a huge bouquet of flowers. "Wow, where did those come from?"

"They are for you honey, so open the wrappings and let's see."

Mair ripped off the paper, "Oh look, Mattie, there must be a couple of dozen red roses. Aren't they beautiful?"

"Who are they from? Look there's a card tucked in the middle of the roses." Mattie pointed out. Mair slowly opened the envelope, took out the card and tears welled in her eyes. She handed the card to Mattie who read it, then said, "Isn't he sweet, Rusty is a fine young man and I hope he'll be able to come back to the states soon."

"I think we are wishing on the stars for that to happen. I sure wish he'd come too, but truthfully, Mattie, I don't have much hope he'll ever come back. His family needs him more than we do." Mair read his letters again, while Mattie went back to the kitchen. Mattie was no sooner gone when she came back to the sun porch.

"Mair, I didn't realize this letter was for you. What does the FBI want with you?" Mattie asked as she handed the letter to Mair. The phone rang and Mattie vias off to answer while Mair opened her FBI letter. She remembered some FBI agents coming to Notre Dame scouting for college students. They were recruiting any student showing interest in joining their school. The letter stated; after their brief talk with MaryRose Gillian at Notre Dame on such and such date and time, the agents were keenly interested in the woman's abilities and academic high grades. They would like to talk further with her. Please contact agent Philip Kern and it gave a phone number.

That night after dinner, Mair showed the letter to her father. "How about that, my daughter a FBI agent." her father smiled.

"Dad, they were talking with anyone walking down the hall who passed by."

"I know dear, but for a lady who likes adventure you might consider the FBI. Did you tell them you were going to Harvard law school in the fall?"

"I don't think so. I talked with them, probably no more than ten minutes and I certainly didn't show any interest."

"My daughter is a FBI agent." Bill said as Mair bent down and kissed him good night. "Wait a minute, honey, sit down here while we have a quiet moment; I've been meaning to talk to you about law school."

How come Dad seeing as I've been accepted. Do you think there is a problem? "Mair asked confused.

"Heaven knows, certainly there is no problem, and I'm excited for you; going to Harvard Law school is truly a challenge. It is extremely difficult, stressful and your time is not yours. I know whatever is put in front of you, no matter how difficult the challenge, you will meet it. My only concern is do you want to spend the next three years meeting these challenges and not sure how you might use them?"

"Dad, you're right to question me. I don't know how I will put the education I receive at Harvard to a viable use, but my reason for going is to learn if the law is what I'm supposed to do. You know I love research and to learn. What better place to do that than Harvard. I need to meet the challenge, in other words."

"Bless you MaryRose; you are one in a million. Don't ever change."

CHAPTER SIX

It didn't take MaryRose long to understand exactly what her Dad meant by Harvard being challenging. Just getting around campus was challenging enough. Going through the tunnels to reach many different buildings was an interesting experience. Harvard has a very large student body. Mair became aware that the first year law students alone were over five hundred, which was divided in sections of 80 students each. MaryRose didn't know a soul in her section, but it didn't take her long to get acquainted with a few.

Her first project was to find living quarters. Most students live off campus. While looking at the maps of possible living quarters to rent she met a girl who seemed just as bewildered as herself Mair moved to the table the gal was sitting at and introduced herself. "Excuse me but you look as lost as I do; I'm MaryRose Gillian, although most call me Mair for short."

"God is good. I really needed to meet someone and yes, I'm completely lost. My name is Nancy O'Mallery." The two girls sat and chatted about their excitement being at Harvard and amazed at the size. "Where do you think we should start looking?" Nancy wondered.

"Well my mother and father both graduated from here and before I left home my Dad pointed out different sections of Cambridge to me...Here is one," Mair pointed.

"Why don't we start there unless you have some insight into another area," Mair suggested.

"Honestly Mair, I'm sure a higher power sent you to me. I'm from the wheat fields of Kansas, and this is the first time in my life I've even been in a big city. I have to admit it scares the wits out of me. So please lead the way." Nancy really sounded relieved. The two girls found a realtor in the area and he showed them a couple of places which seemed okay to the girls, but far from the home they both were used to…even in the wheat fields. After walking what seemed like the entire city, they finally agreed on a place. Mair was excited because it had two bedrooms and two bathrooms, small but adequate.

Nancy was interested in general law, until she found in what part of the law she wanted to major while Mair majored in international law. Most of their classes were different but each enjoyed their little abode and many times, they preferred cooking in their two by four kitchen. Nancy was an excellent cook where Mair was far from it; which reminded her of beloved Mattie and the wonderful meals she prepared every day and night.

Mair being used to going to two masses a week at Notre Dame really missed going to church. The first Sunday she went to St. Paul Church about a block away from Harvard square.

The first mass she heard men and boys sing from the Boston Archdiocesan Choir school. "I could listen to them all day," she told Nancy when she got back to the apartment. "I swear it was like listening to Angels singing from heaven – so inspiring."

"Mair, next Sunday I'd love to go with you and hear them; would that be okay?" Nancy asked.

Nancy did go to mass with Mair more often than not after the first time. Mair asked Nancy what religion she practiced, but she said her family really had no religious background; however, she sure loved to hear the choir at St. Paul's. As time passed, Mair also joined the Harvard Catholic Law Student Association and in time became good friends with the pastor, Father George.

That first year at Harvard passed quickly, with the intention to prepare L-1 students for the bar exam they would eventually take. "Yes, Dad," Mair told her father on one of their frequent phone calls, "you are so right, it's been difficult with so many avenues to go down, but I think I'm holding my own."

"I'm sure you are. Have you decided what your summer work will be and where?"

"I have two interviews next week." Mair said and continued to tell what and where they were. "I wondered if I should go and apply at your firm in DC, but on second thought, I'd be accused of nepotism for sure."

"You're right, but let me know after your interviews how they went. If the firms are smart they'll know a good deal when they see you."

"Dad, I'm also thinking of going to England for my second year law. It certainly would benefit my international law studies, don't you think?"

"Yes, it most likely would if you don't have an alternative motive; with that thought we can end our conversation and I'll say good night my dear." I will never be able to put anything over on that man, bless him. Mair thought smiling as she hung up the phone.

Mair accepted the apprenticeship at the first firm she was interviewed. She liked the attitude and abilities of the law firm itself. Her interviewer was with a woman, probably in her fifties and seemed very interested in MaryRose's application and her knowledge of every question asked.

Being accepted to take her L-2 studies in England at a Harvard's equivalent in Bristol, England presented a problem. She tried hard not to look up on a map as to where

Bristol was in respect to where Rusty lived. Rusty still wrote Mair albeit not as regularly as in the past. In one letter, he did mention there was a law school in Bristol. Mair struggled with the thought of going to law school there and seeing Rusty again. She wasn't sure which was more important to her, and that bothered her. MaryRose always prided herself on being self-assured with a positive attitude. In this incident, she fell short and wished she could visit and talk with Auntie Marge. With that thought, she went to the phone and made an appointment with Father George at St. Paul's. The priest was fond of Mair and glad to hear from her. He agreed to see her Wednesday evening.

The priest and student talk brought out more than her reasoning about Rusty and school in England. Father George had a unique way of getting to the real point of a conversation without, what he called the fluff and feathers. "MaryRose, let's talk about what's really bothering you. You know taking your second year law in Bristol is exciting and something you really want to do, but the fact is it has nothing to do with this young man, Rusty," the priest said. Without letting MaryRose say a word he continued, "Your friend Rusty seems to me is the spoiler. MaryRose love is a strange animal and there is many meanings to the word love – and listening to you talk about Rusty and you wondering if you do love him makes me feel he is someone you care for, like a good friend, but not someone you're in love with. I believe you know you are not in love. So my dear, let's talk about your real problem."

MaryRose listened intensely to Father George. She almost knew what he was about to say before his words were audible. She sat quietly for a few moments taking in what the priest spoke before she said, "Yes Father you're right. I guess I've known for some time I wasn't in love with Rusty."

"If what you say is true, why make problems. Let's face it MaryRose you're too smart to play games, so let's talk about the real problem."

"Three weeks before returning to ND for our senior year, Rusty surprised me by coming to Virginia. We really had a great time together and I was really glad to see him. There was nothing romantic about our relationship and I enjoyed his company; we did fun things together. One night just before he left for Notre Dame, we took a long walk up in the hills. It was a beautiful night and we had walked far from home – we lay down on the side of the Hill – …

"And then," Father George interrupted and said, "You were no longer a virgin."

"Yes," Mair took a deep breath with a sigh of relief, "I've carried the guilt in my heart for a long time always dismissing the lovemaking as being a natural event."

"It is my dear, it is a natural event; do you understand now how guilt can destroy. Let's you and I go into the Chapel and say a few prayers together. The Chapel was dark with just a dim light shining on the cross above the altar. While the two knelt in the dark, a strong feeling of having life in the service of God filled Mair's heart.

As she walked back to the dorm, she thought about her upcoming summer work and then going to England in the fall. Perhaps she would see Rusty if he came to Bristol. Mair came to the realization Rusty was a good friend and not her lover. She hoped they will always have a bond between them. "Oh I feel good," she said aloud to herself as she entered her apartment.

Two days later, she went to McClushen & Todd Law offices in downtown Boston. Their offices were across the street from Nathanial Hall. She was relieved she wouldn't need a car because parking in Boston is nothing more than a giant circus. When MaryRose started her summer job, she was bored at first until she got into the swing of the office and her specific duties of doing research. It changed when she started spending hours in the office file rooms and library researching her particular given project. She actually loved the research and time passed quickly.

MaryRose had one week in between leaving her summer job and boarding the plane for England. As she left church on her last Sunday before her flight, she waited in line of parishioners who wanted to greet Father George. As she got closer to the priest, she suddenly realized the priest was talking with her father and mother. She left her place in line and stood behind her Father giving him a little poke. Father George said, "I think you might turn around." Bill Gillian turned to see his daughter and said, "Fancy meeting you here."

"Dad – Mom why didn't you let me know you were coming? I can't believe you're here, it's so good to see you." Mair said as she hugged them tightly.

"It's wonderful to meet you, Mr. and Mrs. Gillian, but I think this family reunion should move on," the priest suggested as he looked at the remaining parishioners.

"Of course Father, sorry we'll get out of your way," Bill said, "and we'll see you later this evening."

"What's going on? Come and have lunch at my apartment. I haven't got much left, but I have to empty the refrigerator." The Gillians walked arm in arm with Mair between them. As the family ate the variety of leftovers from the refrigerator, Mair was able to get caught up on her family's lives.

"I brought this picture to show you," her Mother said as she handed Mair a picture of Charlyn.

"Oh my heavens! Look at her. She's all grown up and what a beauty," Mair said as tears welled up in her eyes.

"She's taking after her big sister and it is hard to believe she will be sixteen in a few months. By the way, her soccer teammates call her Lyn for short"

"I asked Father George to have dinner with us at the Inn around seven. Should we make a reservation?"

MaryRose had a hectic week after her parents left for Virginia. Getting ready for her flight to England was only a day away. Before MaryRose left, she called her parents to say goodbye again and her Mom told her Rusty called and wanted to know when she would arrive in England? "I did tell him the date and time; I hope I did the right thing Mair, I'm sure you wanted Rusty to know, okay?"

While in flight to England MaryRose wasn't sure whether she was glad her mother told Rusty about the time she would arrive or not. Seven hours later the plane landed – Mair walked across the tarmac leading to the terminal. As passengers entered the terminal you could hear the many greetings, Mair gave a quick glance at the throng of awaiting people, but didn't notice Rusty. She took a deep breath and wasn't sure if she was sorry or glad. "Okay Father George," she thought "which way is it. - I think I'm glad no actually I know I'm glad."

A few minutes passed before her luggage arrived on the baggage ramp and through some shoving and pushing, she was able to grab the suitcase off the ramp. Mair took note of a number of young people her age. One who was near her, Mair stopped and asked, "Excuse me are you possibly going to the University of Bristol?"

"Yes ma'am" she replied in a distinct southern accent. The two women introduce themselves and found out where a cabstand was located. They were waiting in line for the taxi and suddenly, "Mair, Mair, MaryRose," Rusty shouted as he approached carrying a lovely bouquet of flowers.

"I'm so glad I caught you," he said breathlessly. "I have my car here to drive you."

"Rusty, it's so good to see you," Mair said as she gave him a hug and a kiss on the cheek. "I want you to meet my new friend Sally, Sally Ann Jensen." After the introductions, Rusty took both of the girl's hands, gathered their luggage, and led them to his car.

"My car is in the lot on the other side of the terminal. I had a devil of a time finding the space." The ride to the University of Bristol was about sixty miles. The girls had a million questions to ask Rusty about the city of Bristol. You could tell the excitement was rising, as they got closer to the campus. The University was huge with many dormitories spread in all directions. They had to leave Sally off at the accommodation building, as she didn't previously select her dorm. On the other hand, MaryRose did select her dorm months before arriving. After driving around, they finally found Chantry Court, a seven-story building housing only postgraduate students. After going through the admission process, Rusty carried the baggage up to MaryRose's fourth floor studio flat.

"Wow, they advertised the flat as being small and it is, but it is really all I need and look at the big window with its view."

Rusty took a look and said, "It is practically waterfront."

"MaryRose I can't tell you how wonderful it is to see you and I hope we'll be able to spend a lot of time together, but I do have to run now and get back to work. I'll let you get settled and call you on your cell in a few days."

"You look great and it's good to see you again Rusty. Thank you so much for being at the airport and bringing us all the way out here. You always have done special things and yes, we do have a lot to catch up on. I hope we'll be able to get together soon."

Rusty moved close to MaryRose and put his arms around her saying, "Mair, I don't know if we can ever get back what we once had, but I do know, no matter what, we'll always be special friends." He kissed her and left.

The next few days MaryRose explored the campus and the buildings where she would be continuing to learn international law. She was eager to start. There was a common area on each floor of the dorm and students gathered there to chat, debate and generally have a good time. Two days before classes were to begin; she met a young English lad, Drew Phillips. He too was taking many of the international law classes, so they had a lot to agree and disagree about. In the afternoon Drew came by her flat and told her there are great celebrations going on High Street. This Street has many shops; it also led to the waterfront where there were many bars, restaurants, and clubs. Drew said, "how about the two of us do a little celebrating before we have to get down to cracking the books?" It seemed like every law student was on the waterfront and they were definitely celebrating. Drew and Mair crammed themselves into a pub where there was much singing, dancing, and drinking. Mair was not a drinker, although she enjoyed a glass of wine now and again. This particular night she enjoyed quite a few glasses of wine and it wasn't long before she and Drew were singing at the top of their lungs. The next morning, Mair was glad to have a full day to recover and get rid of her headache before classes started the following morning.

CHAPTER SEVEN

As MaryRose's year at Bristol continued, she became more engrossed in international law, primarily in research. It fascinated her and as each part of her research challenged her mind, she never failed to reach the conclusion needed, no matter how long the process took.

Her parents wanted to send her money for a knockabout car. However, Mair thought it would be more practical for her to buy a bicycle. On the campus at Bristol, there must've been a thousand bikes on the streets at any one time. The only time she really needed any kind of transportation was going to church, which was probably less than one mile from her, flat. Mair tried very hard to get to church every Sunday and once during the weekdays. Going to church always gave Mair a sense of peace and well-being.

Rusty called Mair now and again but was only able to see her at the University once during the first four months she was there. He called her the beginning of the fifth month to tell her he had a whole weekend off and would love to spend it with her. MaryRose was delighted feeling she really needed a change. Rusty arrived at noontime on Saturday. MaryRose prepared a quick lunch. Rusty then drove her to the must-see city of Bath. Mair was entranced by the city's beauty and Rusty showed her all the points of interest and then they went to a charming restaurant for dinner. They discussed what was going on in each of their lives and the conversation eventually turned to their relationship. "You know Mair; my love for you runs deep in my heart and always will." Rusty declared.

"Rusty, I love you too, and there were times when I thought it was a romantic love but I realized a while ago my love for you was meant to be between two close friends, and that friendship will be long-lasting." Rusty nodded his head as if he knew that all along.

Rusty admitted he had been dating a girl seriously for the last year. "But then Mair, when you got off the plane in London, I knew the old spark was there." They talked at length about this girl Rusty was dating and it certainly was apparent if nothing else, he certainly was infatuated by her.

"Rusty what we had at Notre Dame was wonderful. I think at that time in our lives we really needed each other and looking back I'm so thankful we had it." They talked for several hours and realized it was getting late, so they drove back to Chantry Court. As soon as MaryRose knew Rusty was coming, she bought a blowup mattress for him to sleep on. However neither one of them got much sleep. They had another glass of wine and talked about what their hopes were for the future. It was three a.m. before either slept. The next morning they walked to church, followed by brunch in one of the restaurants on the waterfront and then Rusty had to head home.

Both Mair and Rusty had taken note of the small attendance at church. Actually, she found very few people at Bristol going to any church. Of all the students she befriended none seem to attend church at all. At one point, she convinced her friend Drew to come to church with her and thereafter he went with her every Sunday.

By now, the Christmas and New Year holidays passed. Although her parents surprised her by coming to spend Christmas with her, the biggest surprise was Mattie came too. Mair was taken back noticing her dear Mattie was getting older, although Mair never knew, or asked for that matter, how old she was. No matter, Mattie arrived with a box full of goodies.

The spring months passed quickly and MaryRose's spare time was limited. She and Drew became good buddies and the little spare time either had, they spent together. Mair suspected Drew might be gay although the subject was never brought up between them, probably because it didn't make any difference anyway.

It was hard to believe the middle of May was already here and in a week, she would be starting her summer job. Dr. Lee, one of her professors, was instrumental in getting her a job doing research at the Cancer Institute of Bristol. It was a large four-story building on the outskirts of Bristol, yet, still close enough to her flat so she could ride her bike to work. The day before she started Dr. Lee called her and asked her to join him and Mrs. Lee for dinner that evening. MaryRose rose was thrilled; she thought Dr. Lee was probably one of the smartest men she ever met, and yet so kind and gentle. MaryRose arrived, at what in America would be called a condo almost ten minutes before her expected arrival. Their condo was beautifully decorated with many Japanese artifacts. Dr. Lee greeted her at the front door, escorted her into the living room, and introduced Mair to his wife. It was obvious Mrs. Lee did not speak English, which surprised MaryRose. Shortly after the introduction, Dr. Lee explained his wife preferred to speak Japanese all the time. He also explained she could speak perfect English, and certainly understood the language. With all the charm of Japanese culture, Mrs. Lee served a delicious dinner. The table was set with chopsticks, which made MaryRose a little uncomfortable. However, it wasn't long before she was presented with silverware. After dinner, MaryRose and Dr. Lee went out on their deck and minutes later, Mrs. Lee came out and served tea and an assortment of Japanese pastries. During this time, Dr. Lee described what MaryRose's job at the Cancer Institute would entail, and he also mentioned the kind of people she would be working with. When desert was over, Dr. Lee walked MaryRose to the front door. MaryRose gave a slight bow to Mrs. Lee, and said, "This has been the most delightful evening I have spent in Bristol. I can't thank you enough." She extended her hand to Mrs. Lee, who in turn took both of her hands and said in English,

"Bless you, my child."

Her work at the Cancer Institute was everything Dr. Lee said it would be. She worked with doctors, scientists, and psychologists all eager to find cures for different types of cancers. MaryRose was definitely in her element.

In the middle of June MaryRose celebrated her 24th birthday and her entire family called to say happy birthday and each had a message of caring. Mair couldn't get over how Chuck's voice had changed and was so deep now. Charlyn, now a typical teenager, cried as she talked to her big sister. Her mother and father told her of their love for her and tremendous pride. Then of course, Mattie got on the phone to share her best wishes with her dear Mair. "Did you get my package," Mattie asked.

"No, what package?" Mair asked. Just then, the doorbell rang and Drew entered carrying a lit birthday cake followed by all the students who lived on Mair's floor. "What in the world – where did this come from?"

"I believe from the lady you're talking to on the phone."

"Mattie, is this the package you were talking about? I really don't have to ask. I can just look at the cake and I know it's from you; it is definitely a Mattie's cake. How in the world did you arrange this?" The room was bursting with so many people that Mair could hardly hear her family on the phone so she told them she would talk to them later and thanked everybody.

When everyone had a piece of Mattie's cake the room emptied. It wasn't long and the phone rang again, "Happy birthday my dear MaryRose."

"Auntie Marge what a wonderful surprise, it is so good to hear your voice. I got your card yesterday. I sat for a long time looking at the convent chapel and wishing I was there, praying with you." The two women talked for a few more minutes more and then it was time to end the call. Mair walked over to her desk where the card was and sat there just looking at the convent chapel. Looking at the card brought back all the desires of leading a religious life. She immediately took out some writing paper and wrote a note to Auntie Marge jotting down all her thoughts. She told her aunt that religious life at the University of Bristol was practically nonexistent, and she missed that life. She wrote about Rusty and their meeting of the minds and she told her about Dr. Lee and his wife, and all that he had done for her. She also wrote that it would be good to get home to America and take her last year of law school.

She met so many talented people working at the Cancer Institute and was surprised to see many of them were quite young, certainly a group of dedicated people to their cause. MaryRose was amazed at how much she was learning about not only cancer, but also the intricate details of research.

Her friend Drew had a rather old car he treasured and he and MaryRose went exploring England on the weekends, at least the ones they weren't working. Drew and his family lived in Italy although they were US citizens, and evidently had a home in Arizona. As time went on, Mair found Drew and his family life very interesting. Having seen a good deal of the English countryside, he was able to show MaryRose some very interesting places. She fell in love with the English countryside and enjoyed their adventures. Drew was able to not only tell her, but also show her so much of England's history. He became a good friend to MaryRose. He didn't ask anything of her, only her friendship and the two had a great deal of fun together.

It was only a matter of three weeks when MaryRose's time at the University of Bristol would be over. In retrospect, it was well worthwhile, and she sadly would have to say goodbye again. She made many friends on her flat floor and the one special friend, Drew. Their goodbye would be difficult; the two really became good life-long friends

Mair already had her plane reservations going directly to Washington DC. She wanted to spend a week with her family before leaving for her L-3 year at Harvard. Even before leaving England though, Mair planned on spending one of her three weeks in London. Drew had shown her many interesting places in England, but she really wanted to see more of London. She called Rusty to tell him she would be there and did he have time to see her. "Of course I will." Rusty replied, "I knew the time was close when you would be going back to the USA and with your call today I'll be able to make arrangements to see you and maybe you'll get to meet Tina, the girl I told you I was dating."

"That would be great. So give me a call to let me know which day will work for you. I just can't leave without seeing you and saying goodbye."

"That sounds so final, M-Rose."

"Wow I haven't heard anyone call me that name in years." MaryRose said, "but you know Rusty, we might yet see each other again. Once I start working in international law, who knows where you might find me."

She no sooner got off the phone and it rang again. It was the Chancellor's secretary. It seems the Chancellor wanted to see her as soon as possible, meaning today. To say the least, MaryRose was surprised and puzzled. She never heard of the Chancellor wanting to see any student, so why her? Mair showered and dressed quickly and was on her way to the administration building. The Chancellor's office was on the second floor. It was seldom a student was asked to even go up to the second floor, so this was new territory to MaryRose. She announced herself to a woman seated behind a huge desk. "Oh yes, Miss Gillian. Titular Chancellor Howard will see you now," she said as she pointed to his door. Mair obviously had been announced as Chancellor Howard was waiting at his door.

"Miss Gillian, thank you for being so prompt, please come in," By this time MaryRose was completely bewildered. "I first want to congratulate you on your outstanding work and studies here at the University. Secondly, I must admit I was anxious to meet you; your name has come to the attention of this office numerous times, so many times it was imperative I meet you."

"Thank you, Sir"

The man nodded and continued, "There is a young man in our conference room, who asked to speak to you. He is an FBI agent and according to him, you know him. His name is Philip Kern. It is true you do, in fact, know Mr. Kern?"

Rather than go into any detail MaryRose chose to say, "Yes." She remembered talking to an FBI agent, but she didn't remember his name. However, she thought she might remember his looks. The Chancellor walked her to the door, which evidently led to the room where Mr. Kern was waiting to talk to her. At first glance she did recall seeing this man before. He was the agent who spoke to her at Notre Dame, again at Harvard and even in Virginia at her home.

Most of their previous conversations were very casual talking about if she had any interest in becoming an agent.

"How are you Miss Gillian. It's been a while?"

"You know, Mr. Kern, I think it's time we sat down and have a long talk." MaryRose said. "I am getting the feeling that I'm being followed and I really don't like the feeling. I think I'm beginning to resent your intrusion."

"I do agree we should talk. I'd like to prove to you I'm not really the villain you might think I am. I would like very much for you to accept invitation to have dinner with me tonight."

"Look, Mr. Kern…

"Please call me Phil." He interrupted.

"Okay, but you don't have to take me to dinner; I just want to know what is your purpose. Each time you asked me if I'd be interested to become an FBI agent. I believe, or at least I thought I made it very clear that I wasn't interested. For some reason and I'd love to know the reason why you're so persistent?"

"Please believe me, Miss Gillian I want you to know all of my reasons for pursuing and most likely bothering you. There are things I want to tell you, but not here." There was a knock on the door and the Chancellor stuck his head in.

"I'm sorry to interrupt you. However, we are about to walk out now so I'm afraid I will have to ask you to leave. I am frightfully sorry for this inconvenience."

MaryRose spoke up before Phil could say anything, "Chancellor Howard, it is perfectly all right. We were about to leave anyway." Immediately Phil got up from his chair at the same time as MaryRose. Once on the sidewalk Phil said, "The best place to speak freely is outside in open-air. In other words, I don't want anybody to hear this but you. How about we go sit on the park bench over there?"

"Well, if nothing else, you certainly have aroused my curiosity, so yes let's go sit on the park bench."

"We, the FBI, get from practically every college in the USA lists of students that excel not only scholastically but in character, sociability, reliability and the list goes on. When I got the list from Notre Dame, your name was at the top of every list. Harvard University had the same results – you exceeded everyone else as you did here at the University of Bristol. Miss Gillian the Bureau needs people with your credentials, so it became my job to convince you to become an FBI agent. We know you've been studying international law. We also know your investigative powers are beyond reproach."

"Phil, I know you most likely know I'm going back to Harvard for my third year law and that will conclude seven years of school…" She hesitated for a minute or two, so Phil broken in,

"Do you mind if I asked you what are your plans after the seven years?"

"I don't know, and I must admit that bothers me. What I would like to do after law school is take time off to find out what's next for me.

"May I call you MaryRose?"

"By all means Phil, in fact, you can call me Mair, if you like."

"Mair? Where did that come from?" Phil asked

"Well my little sister had a hard time saying MaryRose so Charlyn, my little sister, started calling me Mair, which is pronounced like fair and before long the whole family called me Mair.

"I don't know about you Mair, but I'm really hungry. How about we go get something to eat?"

"Sounds good to me, Phil." The two had a very nice dinner together and somehow MaryRose's resentments toward the man seemed to fade. Phil walked her to her flat and before saying goodbye, he handed her his business card.

"Take this card, and if you ever want to get in touch with me please free to do so."

Early the next morning, MaryRose checked her list of "to-do." First on her list was to call Rusty and let him know what day she would be in London. Even though she would see Rusty just to say goodbye because of his schedule, she was also anxious to meet Tina. Rusty said since it was a working day he thought it best that they meet for lunch and Tina might be able to come too. The next on her list was to stop by the lab and see Dr. Lee. He was glad to see her even though he knew it was a goodbye call. Before MaryRose left, Dr. Lee reached into his pocket and took out a small box, beautifully wrapped and handed it to her saying, "Mrs. Lee wanted you to have this little token to remember us. Good luck, MaryRose and I have a feeling you're going to great places and will accomplish wonderful things. If possible, both Mrs. Lee and I would love to hear from you."

When MaryRose got back to her flat, she looked around the room, and wondered where to start.

She organized her clothes and packed them in her suitcase. Then she went around the room and collected little things - pens, pencils, file folders and pads, as well as the desk lamp she had bought and put them in a cardboard box. MaryRose carried the box down the hall and knocked on Drew's door. He opened the door and said, "My look at all those goodies all for me. Come on in MaryRose. We have about a half-hour before we have to leave for the airport."

"I'm really going to miss our flat friends on this floor. I got to say goodbye to almost everyone, I don't think I missed anybody. But I'll miss you Drew, most of all."

"That reminds me," Drew said as he went over to his desk, "here MaryRose this is my home address, I think that's where I'll be after next year when I graduate. Even if I'm not living at home, my parents will surely know where I am."

"What makes you think I'll be back in England anytime soon?"

"Somehow, my friend, I really do think you'll be in Europe many times over. And even if you're not, you could write once in a while. And now my lady friend, I think we should be on the road to the airport." They both were quiet on the twenty-five minute trip to the airport. Once there, they said their goodbyes and Marr bordered the plane to London.

MaryRose was glad it was a short trip to Heathrow airport. As soon as MaryRose deplaned and walked into the terminal she spotted Rusty and rushed over to him. She received a big hug and kiss from Rusty. He took her arm and escorted her to his car saying, "M-rose it is so good to see you although I am sad that you'll be leaving England shortly."

"You know Rusty, it's always good to see you and hopefully in the future we will see each other now and again. But Rusty, I thought that Tina was going to be with us?"

"Well, that's kind of a long story; I'll tell you about it when we get to the restaurant." It wasn't very long before they reached the pub where Rusty chose to have lunch. Once settled at their table and ordering their food, Rusty told M-rose that he and Tina had broken up. From what Rusty said evidently Tina wasn't willing to wait for a long period of time before they got married. "You know M-rose I finally am getting my feet on the ground. I have gotten a good job, but it's going to take time for me to make a substantial salary. I still have to add to the support of my mother and siblings so I feel marriage right now is out of the question." MaryRose, was sad to hear this and told him she hoped in time they'd be able to work things out. "MaryRose, I hate to have to rush our lunch together, but I have to get back to work." He drove MaryRose to a cab stand and their goodbyes were quick.

The next few days MaryRose spent being a true tourist in London. She got to see all the wonderful things she had read about and always wanted to see. In no time though, it was time for her to go back to the airport and fly to Virginia. Once on the plane, she promised herself she would be back one day to enjoy London again.

The eight hour trip passed quickly to Washington DC. Mair was excited she would see her family in just a few more hours. She dozed off wondering what her life would be after graduating from Harvard.

CHAPTER EIGHT

MaryRose's excitement was on a high with the prospect of seeing her family in a few moments. As her plane landed at Dulles International Airport, she tried to make an effort to be the first off the plane. Mair rushed to enter the airport terminal and there waiting for her was her Mother, Father, Mattie, Chuck with a strange girl, and her not so little sister, Charlyn. It was a wonderful reunion with hugs and kisses all around. As they walked to the baggage claim, Mair inched closer to Chuck and whispered, "Who is the girl?"

"Oh, I'm sorry. Mair, this is Christine." Chuck said and smiled broadly. They all piled into her dad's car except Chuck and Christine who followed in Chuck's new sports car. It was dinnertime when they pulled into the Gillian driveway and as they reached the kitchen door Mair could smell her favorite meal. She immediately went over to Mattie, gave her a big hug, and said, "Thank you Mattie you are such a dear." The conversation at the dinner table went on until ten o'clock that night. All MaryRose could think of is how wonderful it was to be with her family in her home.

The next morning she went into the kitchen and her mother sitting at the table said, "Dad had to run in to Washington for a little while, but he'll be home this afternoon."

"Mom, it is so good to be here and I'll be glad to wait until Dad comes home. I'm going to treasure every moment I have in these next three days."

"I know dear. It's such a short time, but we'll make the best of every minute. Is there anything special you would like to do?

"No, Mom, not really. It seems I've been on the go for the last year and having nothing to do is a special treat."

Those three days seemed to fly by, but Mair enjoyed every minute. She had long talks with Charlyn, though she must remember she is called Lyn these days. They talked about Lyn being on the girl's high school soccer team and Mair's old teammate, Carol was now Lyn's head coach. Mair also talk to Chuck, but not necessarily long talks. It seems Chuck and his girlfriend Christine have been dating for almost a year and the parents believe it might be serious. Mair did ask if he and Christine had any future plans but all she could get out of Chuck was that Christine was one great gal. Mair surmised all that meant was it's none of her business. Her last day at home was Sunday, and of course, the family went to Saint Anne's for mass. They hadn't told Father Paul Mair was coming home because they weren't sure she would be able to see him. When Father Paul was giving his homily, it was obvious he spotted MaryRose in the congregation. When mass was over the Gillians stayed seated in their pew until the rest of the parishioners filed out and greeted Father Paul. As soon as the greetings were over Father rushed back into the church and greeted the Gillian family. When he came to MaryRose, he stood back and just looked at her and finally said, "It's a dream come true to see you. Mair. You look wonderful." Before anyone else could say a thing Bill Gillian said, "I made reservations at the Inn downtown. Chuck, help Father clean up sacristy and we'll meet you there in fifteen minutes."

The Gillian household was sad the next morning when once again, they were saying goodbye to Mair.

"Just remember after this year, I most likely will be around for a long time," Mair noted.

"Who knows what next year will bring my dear, but it sure would be great to have you here or at the very least, nearby," her Dad remarked as he drove her to the airport to catch her flight to Boston.

"Oh Dad, before I forget, I forgot to tell Mom that I spoke to Jenna, you know my Notre Dame roommate and their new baby girl is named Rose; she's only two months old, but pictures will be coming soon."

Mair's L1 roommate, Nancy was at the Boston airport to drive her back to Harvard. Nancy and Mair really have a good relationship and missed each other while Mair was in England, and were glad to see each other again. They both are looking forward to their L3 year because it was the end of their schooling, but more exciting is looking forward to be able to practice law. They spent the rest of the afternoon and well into the evening catching up on each other's lives.

Both girls found their L3 year very intense and they had little time to do anything else but stick with their studies. It wasn't until the end of April things loosened up a bit and all the talk was about graduation and more importantly where they could find work as a lawyer. It was at this time many law offices in Boston were scouting possible law students for their firms. Mair was presented offers even before the interview. No matter, she still was determined to take one year off with no commitments.

There were seven hundred plus students graduating and Mair wanted to be sure her parents made reservations well ahead of time. Mair would be able to get the three tickets needed for both class day on May twenty-ninth and commencement day, May thirtieth. Her parents, along with Mattie made reservations at the Prudential and would arrive on the twenty-sixth of May. Classes were actually over by May fifth, so neither Nancy nor Mair could imagine the chaos to follow. There were U-Haul trucks or trailers all over the place as students cleared out the dorms. Students were renting out beds in their L2 dormitories for graduates to have someplace to sleep until their parents arrive affording better accommodations. The drinking and partying were rampant, but nothing that matched the Barrister Ball, which started early evening and didn't end until two a.m. and drinks were on the house. Further details necessarily are not needed. However, it made it almost impossible to come on the campus area, so Mair met her parents at the hotel.

At six forty-five a.m. on class day there was a sunrise breakfast for students and their families if they wished. At seven-fifteen a.m. the morning of class day, the classes prepared to march into the theater, led by the Dean. The University came at nine forty-five and the law graduates marched in at eleven forty-five a.m.. At the class day ceremonies, awards and prizes were presented and MaryRose Gillian received both awards and prizes for her outstanding successes in law school. The following day was commencement day with all the pomp and circumstances. Mattie and the Gillians were extremely proud of their daughter's accomplishments.

It had been an exhausting week for all concerned, and the Gillians were glad to be on the road back to Virginia. They left Boston the day after graduation and planned to drive straight through to Virginia. Ordinarily they would've taken two days, but Marianne Gillian had to be at the Georgetown graduation the next day.

The first week MaryRose was home she lounged around the house, straightened out her room from all the unpacking and found room for the multitude of books she had acquired. Towards the end of the week, she took Lyn and one of her friends to the beach. She relished the day with her little sister, although she knew she couldn't say that anymore as Lyn was only an inch shorter than Mair. It was a fun day and she realized what a lovely young lady Lyn became.

It was just about a week later when Mair got a phone call from Phil Kern. She was almost disappointed it didn't come earlier as she found she was not only expecting it, but wishing he would call. "Hey there MaryRose. How is life treating you with no class to go to?"

"Hey there yourself. Who are you hounding these days? Where are you?"

"Well, most of the colleges have had graduations so right now I haven't much to do to tell truth."

"Oh, I find that hard to believe, Mr. Phil. An FBI man idle at his desk; I don't think that looks very good." They both laughed, knowing full well it wasn't the case.

"What about you? I find it hard to believe this award-winning law graduate from Harvard is sitting idle either."

"To tell you the truth Phil, I'm so damn idle I'm bored stiff."

"I'm sure MaryRose it's difficult to wind down after the whirlwind you've been on the last year. So let me help you relax. How about coming into town and having dinner with me soon?"

"Well, aren't you the gallant man trying to save the lady in distress from going nuts." MaryRose paused for a few seconds before saying, "Maybe that's what I need, but you have to make one promise."

"And my dear lady, what could that be?"

"You don't ask me what my plans are for this year. Is it a deal?"

"You can bet on it; you have a deal." They made plans where and when to meet on Friday. At first Phil wanted to come and pick her up at the house, but she pooh-poohed that idea and said she would drive into DC. The truth was she didn't want anybody in the family to think this was a date. Just then Chuck and Christine came in asking her to come out and play doubles tennis.

"How are we going to play doubles with three?" Mair asked.

"No, there's someone to surprise you outside who wants to play with us." Mair asked them to wait a minute, and ran upstairs to change her clothes, all the while wondering who could be the surprise fourth player. She came down stairs and when she got to the back porch she still couldn't see anybody else on the tennis court, except Chuck and Christine. She didn't see anyone when she got to the tennis court either.

"I guess the fourth player is the Phantom." Mair said as she looked around.

"The Phantom I'm not." A voice came from behind her. Mair quickly turned.

"Oh my heavens, can that be you, Tom Tyson. I haven't seen you – I don't know how many years it's been."

"I've certainly heard great things about you, Mair. Chuck has kept me updated on all your accolades."

"Tom, how are you and your wife. Do you have any children?"

"Hold on Mair, one question at a time. We have two children, a boy and a girl, and Maria is okay, and I'm doing pretty well." Although Mair hadn't seen Tom in many years, she could tell he wasn't the happy-go-lucky guy she remembered. But then she thought he is after all a grown man and a father now.

"Come on guys, let's get this game started, or we'll be playing in the dark," Chuck called to them. Mair had forgotten Chuck and Tom played tennis regularly and have for years. They had her running in a very tight game. However, they all enjoyed playing, which included much laughter as they expended a great deal of energy, but had plain fun. Even Mair felt for sure she'd be stiff come tomorrow morning. Chuck asked Tom to stay for dinner, but he said he had to leave as he was expected at home. Mair was sorry she didn't get a chance to talk more with Tom but did ask Chuck if Tom was unhappy.

"I don't know about that Mair. I asked him the same question and he avoids answering, so I let it go. The talk around town is the happy marriage has turned sour, if you can believe the talk around town."

"I hope it is all talk. Tom's a real nice guy."

"You're right and I wish there was something I could do for him," Chuck commented.

"You can Chuck – just be a good friend," his big sister advised.

As Mair entered the back door she called to Mattie she was going up stairs to take a shower. Mattie came to the bottom of the stairs and told her that a Phil Kern called and will call her back after the dinner hour.

"I can't tell you how wonderful it is to have all six of us sitting around the dinner table. It's been a long time and I have to admit I missed it," Bill remarked to his children. He said grace before meals and Mair thanked God for her family. As her Mother and Mattie were serving dessert the phone rang. Mattie looked at Mair and said she might as well get the phone because it was probably Phil calling back. It was Phil telling Mair the place and time to meet in DC.

As Mair and Phil were being escorted to their table at the posh 1789 restaurant in Georgetown, heads turned to look at this attractive couple being seated. Her mother often talked about 1789 restaurant as being one of the finest restaurants in DC; however, Mair had never been there. As she looked around she understood what her mother meant by it is classy.

When seated, Phil ordered a bottle of the best champagne offered. When Mair tasted the champagne she said, "mmm, this is delicious. I can see what they mean; this is certainly the best champagne I've ever tasted." They ordered dinner and Phil asked Mair to dance. Mair just couldn't understand why she felt so comfortable with this man, who she claimed not to like at all. They talked at great length over dinner and wine, mostly about their families and where and how they grew up. Phil kept his word and never mentioned Mair's year off to figure what she wanted to do next.

After a delicious dinner, they had coffee and a cordial, talked endlessly, danced and laughed and before they left, it was almost midnight.

Once outside Phil asked, "There's a little café around the corner, how about we have a big cup of black coffee?"

"I think it's a great idea. Standing out in this fresh air I really feel a little wobbly. I guess I'm not used to drinking. I think the coffee is good idea, but first let's just take a walk. It's such a beautiful night and I think the fresh air will be just as beneficial right now as a cup of coffee." Mair took Phil's arm mainly to steady herself, and they took a long walk around Georgetown University before they headed to the Café.

"Does this café stay open all night? It's well after midnight now," Mair wondered.

"Mair, I hope your parents aren't worried. I don't want them to think I kidnapped you." Phil said concerned.

"You know Phil, I've been away from home for so long I don't even think my parents worry about me anymore. Maybe I should call home and let it ring a couple of times, and then leave a message. Thanks for bringing it up, I guess for parents it's hard to think I'm not the little girl anymore."

"I think you're right. To our parents we're always their children no matter what our age. Before you call though, why don't we get you a room for tonight? I'm not a parent Mair, but I think I would worry having you drive through the city and into Virginia at this time of night."

Mair laughed and said, "I didn't know you cared." Before Phil could answer they were at the all-night café. They both were amazed how crowded it was and Phil said,

"I think we're getting old and forgetting that young people think midnight is very early at least too early to go home." They were lucky enough to get a booth way in the back corner of the Café and had to wait a while to get waited on. Somehow waiting didn't seem to bother them. Mair excused herself and went to the ladies room, not to use the ladies room, but to call home. In order not to wake anyone in the house she decided to text them. She simply wrote she was spending the night in DC and not to worry she would call them first thing in the morning.

When Mair returned to the table, she told Phil she had text messaged her parents. He looked relieved. They ordered their coffee along with the café specialty, crumb cake. Their conversation turned personal when it was Mair who asked, "Phil, how come a good looking guy like you isn't married."

Probably the same reason a beautiful lady like you isn't married," he laughed and then continued, "I'm kidding the truth is Mair I was married for three and a half years when my wife died of breast cancer."

"Oh I'm so sorry. I had no right to even ask the question."

"Yes, you did Mair and the only reason why I didn't and won't ask you the same question is because I know why you didn't marry."

"Because of my going to school?" she asked. Phil nodded and laid his hand on top of Mair's. She did not resist and continued, "School was all consuming to me and while I did date, although I must admit not very often, as I told you before, I don't know where the future will lead me." They sat for probably another hour and Phil told her about his wife. They had no children. She developed cancer, actually right after their honeymoon, so there was little time to even make a baby. Mair told Phil about her relationship with Rusty she laughed and said,

"Actually it was a very short relationship, but I will always be fond of him. He is a neat guy, married and happy. And now you really do know my life story."

"I'm glad. You are a very interesting woman and I hope to even learn more about you." Mair smiled and commented how there was still a large crowd in the Café and it was almost three AM. "I guess we better go find you a room." "

"I think that's a good idea," Mair said as she stood up, ready to leave. I probably could find something around Georgetown to stay for the night," MaryRose said as they left the restaurant.

"The FBI has a block of rooms at the Sheraton hotel and there are several rooms I know are vacant. Why don't I give the Sheraton a call and make sure there's still some available. You can take one of those rooms, no problem."

"Is that allowed?" Mair questioned, "with no strings attached to the deal, right?" Before Mair got the words out of her mouth, Phil was on his cell phone making the arrangements. He hailed a taxi for the short ride to the hotel. It dawned on Mair she had no idea where Phil lived so asked, "by the way Phil where do you live?"

"Oh, I have a little house, actually a cottage on the outskirts of Washington. Well here we are; I'll come in to make sure the reservation is made, and everything is right." There was hardly a soul in the lobby, but then it was three-thirty in the morning. Phil checked her in and led her to the elevator. He handed her keys to her room and took both of her hands in his, "MaryRose I hope you find whatever you're looking for and enjoy this year of searching. If you ever need anything, you know where you can find me." They stood just looking at each other hand-in-hand for a moment or two before the elevator door opened. MaryRose entered, and as the door started to close Phil held them open with his hands for a minute before letting the door close.

MaryRose felt Phil's urge to kiss her, because she had the same urge. She got in bed quickly but didn't sleep very well. Her thoughts were all over the place knowing she had feelings for Phil and those feelings confused her more.

Mair only slept about an hour. She opened her eyes, just wide enough to see the clock which read eight-fifteen a.m. She quickly got up and called home. Mattie answered and MaryRose told her she would be home probably within the next hour and a half. Mattie seemed more than glad to hear from her, which allowed Mair to think there might've been some talk about her not coming home. She dressed quickly and went downstairs to the front desk to check out.

"I'm Miss Gillian, and I'd like to check out."

"Oh yes, Miss Gillian, Mr. Kern was here earlier and brought your car keys. He said the car is parked right out front and asked me to give you this envelope." A stunned Mair almost gasped, realizing both she and Phil forgot her car in Georgetown.

"Thank you so much may I have my bill?" The clerk informed her Mr. Kern took care of the bill, so she was all set to go. MaryRose got in her car and as she pulled away from the curb, she found herself looking around in case Phil was close by.

When she got home, Mattie and her Mom were in the kitchen having breakfast. They didn't ask her any questions which MaryRose appreciated. She did tell them she had dinner at the 1789 club and how her Mother was right telling her it was excellent. She got a bite to eat and went up to her room to take a shower. While getting ready she heard her Mom coming up the stairs. "Mom, can you come in my room for a minute?" Her mother entered and MaryRose said, "Mom, do you think it would be possible for me to go up to the convent and see Auntie Marge and maybe stay for a couple of days or weeks. I don't know, all I do know, I need help."

"Can I help you, sweetheart?" Her Mom asked.

"Oh, Mom you are always my strength and I can only hope to be just as successful and strong and understanding and loving as you are. You are my role model. Now I need to get away from everything that's familiar and find what direction I'm going; find what's next for me. I'm hoping at the convent I can finally figure things out and what direction God want me to follow?" The two women hugged each other and her Mom said she would call Marge this morning.

CHAPTER NINE

The following morning MaryRose arrived to the welcome arms of her Auntie Marge. Her emotions got the best of her and her aunt held her close. Mair cried. She was as surprised as Auntie Marge. As Mair dried her tears, she remarked, "Auntie Marge, I haven't cried like that since I can't remember when, I just couldn't control it."

"My dear, a good cry can cure a lot of things. Now come let's go to my dining room and have a marvelous lunch the sisters have prepared for us. The two women chatted mostly about family while they ate, although Mair had a million things she wanted to talk to her aunt about. When lunch was over, they strolled through the gardens and sat down in the arbor covered in rosebuds. The fragrant air was overwhelming. Mair commented, "This is just a little bit of paradise."

"Yes, isn't it? It really is sent directly from heaven. Mair I have to tell you, you look wonderful but tired."

"Thank you and you're right, I am tired. I found out law school takes a heck of a lot of energy. It was sometimes draining but I must admit I really enjoyed Harvard and the University of Bristol."

"Yes, I'm sure you found England fascinating. It has so much history, especially of the old world. And did you see the young man you were interested in at Notre Dame?"

"Oh, I have so much to tell you, I really don't know where to begin. But first of all don't let me take you away from attending to your duties to the sisters and nuns." The Mother Superior assured her niece she wouldn't interfere with any of her responsibilities. They sat in the arbor for the better part of the afternoon talking about Mair's experiences in law school.

At one point in their conversation, Mother Superior had some business to attend. In the meantime Mair walked in the gardens and met a couple of the nuns and several novices. They all seemed to know who she was and Mair enjoyed speaking with them. She did make note how very young the novices she met were. One approached and asked MaryRose to come with her to the dining room. When all were seated and the prayers said, there really wasn't much conversation between them. MaryRose wondered why or is it part of their way they live. With dinner finished all the women proceeded to the chapel where evening vespers were sung. Mair wondered how in the world she would fit in the convent because she couldn't even carry a tune, and these women's voices were like angels. With vespers over Mair caught Auntie Marge's eye who motioned her to follow to her office. First thing Mair asked was does she have the same voice as her sister. The nun quietly replied, "Yes I'm afraid I do."

"Wow, how could you become Mother Superior and not be able to sing like an opera star? I thought that was a prerequisite." And they both laughed.

"Mair, your Mother said you would like to spend a few days or more here at the convent. What are your plans?'

"My plans? I wish I knew my plans. Auntie Marge, I wanted to come to the convent to be with you and try to find myself and my plans. You always have so much insight into people, certainly into me. With all my book knowledge and accolades, I really have no idea where I'm headed, and I have to tell you, it bothers me immensely. Yes I do want to spend some time at the convent. I want the peace, I want the prayer and I want the guidance. If it would be better for me to go to the motel in town for the night, that's perfectly all right. I just want to be in a place close to God. Just going to the chapel this evening I found such peace. I need peace, but not just in the chapel I need peace in my life.

"My dear, you are welcome to stay here in the convent for as long as you like and you think you need. We have some rooms here that are empty. They're not as fine as even the downtown motel but they're adequate. Come with me and let's get you settled."

They went to an upper floor that had long corridors with every twelve or so feet doors to enter. The halls were shiny clean, like they never had been walked on. Several doors from the staircase Auntie Marge opened a door. Mair had never seen any of the rooms the nuns occupied. The room had a window covered with spanking white curtains, a small bed, a four drawer chest, a bed stand with a lamp and one drawer with a shelf on the bottom, a writing table at the end of the bed and a small sink with a cabinet above, but no mirror. Right as you entered the room there was a closet, a small closet. Mair surmised there was a large room with a bath or shower somewhere on the floor. With Mair and her aunt in the room it was crowded. As Mair looked around the room her aunt said, "This is it, or would you want to go the hotel downtown?"

"Absolutely not, I'll stay right here."

"MaryRose, tomorrow I have pretty busy schedule, at least in the morning so you do whatever you please and I'll see you at lunch time. In the meantime, you know that you're welcome to go in the library, the chapel, where ever, and of course, the gardens. If you choose to leave the grounds let Sister Joel know. Goodnight my dear and God love you.

MaryRose fell easily into the routine of the novices. She ate with them, prayed with them and worked with them. She was happiest being in the garden. Most were very young, but there was one woman who probably was in her forties. Mother Superior had explained to all the visitor was her niece and would be staying with them for a little while. No one seemed to mind, in fact, in a short time it seemed they were one happy family.

Auntie Marge was able to spend a great deal of time with Mair, spending hours talking. "I asked you before if you got to see the young man you met at Notre Dame while you were in England?"

"Oh, yes, several times, and it was good to see him. He's doing very well, has a good job and is planning on getting married, I think."

"You think what does mean - think?" Mair explained that Tina was supposed to have lunch with Rusty and me, but Tina was a no-show.

"Rusty was really pretty vague about the whole situation and obviously he didn't want to talk about her. Something like she wanted to get married right away but he wanted to wait until he was more settled."

"Did you feel he had any interest in you anymore?"

"No, not really. Sometimes it sounded like he might like to, but actually it was apparent to both of us, what we had in the past was in fact past." Mair told her aunt about her friend Drew and Dr. Lee. She was there a couple weeks before she mentioned Phil, and then only briefly. The nun must've noticed something when she talked about Phil because some weeks later she asked,

"Tell me more about the young man, Phil."

"Oh him? Mair questioned, "When I was in my last year at Notre Dame he was the guy who was the FBI recruiter. He stopped me and handed me some literature, and asked me a couple questions. I saw him again at Harvard and even in England at Bristol, then again, my third year at Harvard. When he showed up in England, I really was annoyed thinking this guy is following me all over the globe

"Knowing you I suppose you told him to get lost."

"Well I told him in so many words I wasn't interested in the FBI, so all his efforts were in vain. Actually, I did bargain with him. If he left me alone I'd go out to lunch with him."

"That's very interesting," Auntie Marge commented.

"You really think so? I thought he was one pain in the neck."

"Well, that evidently wasn't the end of him because you saw him again at Harvard, right?"

"I did, and after graduation he called me in Virginia, at the house mind you, and wanted to take me out to dinner."

"I have a feeling MaryRose you went out to dinner with this young man," her aunt guessed.

"Yes – I did and it was quite a night and I'll spare you any details."

"Are you in love?" Mair did not answer, rather she quickly got up from her chair and rushed out the door to the garden. Her aunt's reaction was to think yes, she is involved. The nun had several appointments in the afternoon so she started to go to her office, but stopped for a moment at the chapel first. She prayed and asked God to help MaryRose find her way or better still to find His way. A young girl was waiting for her outside of her office. The nun welcomed her and they went into her office.

MaryRose and her aunt did not see each other again until the evening meal. MaryRose was waiting by the entry to the dining room when the Mother Superior arrived. She gave her aunt a hug and quietly said, "I'm sorry." Her aunt smiled broadly and they walked to their places in the dining room. After dinner and the beautiful vespers, Auntie Marge asked Mair to join her in her lounge. When they were alone, the first thing MaryRose did was to apologize to her aunt for her actions earlier in the day. "I really am sorry. I acted like a child having a tantrum. I guess Auntie Marge you hit a nerve and it sent me flying.

"My dear niece, you don't owe me any apology. I probably was asking questions I had no business to ask. Your personal life is just that – personal. You know I'll listen to anything you have to say."

"The problem is you always know the answers before I do. It bothers me I don't know them when I should. Auntie Marge, it's the same old story; you asked if I'm in love, and the reason I didn't answer is because I don't know. That night in Washington DC when Phil and I had dinner together was one of the happiest nights I can remember. I felt free. I felt cared for and I felt emotions. You know I seldom do or I seldom have felt emotions." Tears roll down Mair's cheek and before she could say another word the nun put her finger to Mair's lips.

"You see my dear you are feeling emotions right now. Those emotions brought the tears rolling down your cheek," the older woman gently said.

"Then why – why do I suppress them, why am I afraid to show them? You know full well my mother and father are emotional and easily show their feelings towards each other and everybody."

"MaryRose I can't give you all the answers. These are the answers that are within you. If you need help finding them, get the help. Don't be afraid. You might be surprised. In fact, I know you will." MaryRose sat there for a minute, taking in all that her aunt said and realized there were really very few moments in her life she let her emotions show to anyone with the exception possibly to her immediate family.

"It's like a stroke of lightning," the young woman said.

"What is MaryRose?"

"It wasn't like I learned something for the first time. I sat there right in front of you and realized I must feel weak if I cry or yell or do anything I think is not normal for fear I'll show my weaknesses and not be strong. I really think that is part of my problem, and it's hard to believe I never thought or felt that before – my dear Auntie Marge, you always bring out the best in me."

"No, my child, you bring out the best in yourself. Look at all the good you've done in your young life. You excelled in everything you wanted to do and if you want to share your emotions you'll be a winner again. I know you will."

"Auntie Marge, I'm going to go home. You've been so generous with your time, but it is time I face what is real. It is time I show to my brother and little sister that I love them and show them I do care what is going on in their lives. It is true – right- that it is all right to be wrong?"

"Oh yes, that is how we learn to be right."

MaryRose arrived home late the next afternoon and was disappointed not to find a soul at home. She unlocked the front door and called to see if anybody would answer her, but heard not a sound. She went to her room and unpacked her clothes and put aside the dirty ones. She went downstairs and put her dirty clothes in the washing machine. Just as she turned the machine on, she thought she heard someone call out, "Who is there?"

"Is that you MaryRose?"

"Yes Mattie," Mair said as she walked into the kitchen and gave Mattie a huge hug and kiss. "We didn't know you were coming home today, did we?"

"No, Mattie, I decided I would surprise everybody. I had a wonderful time with Auntie Marge, but she is a busy lady and six weeks is a long time to have a visitor – plus the fact I missed seeing you guys. By the way, where is everybody?"

"Well, your mom and dad are still at work and Chuck and Christine are probably at her house, checking out all their wedding plans. I have to tell you Mair, that girl is going to wear your brother out; she has him running all over the place. I think Lyn went to the church, Father Paul is keeping those young ones busy this summer."

"And how Miss Mattie are you?" Mattie didn't answer. Mair at first wondered if she heard her, however she did notice or thought Mattie was slowing down and looked a little pale. She decided she would check it out with her mom later. She moved closer to Mattie and asked her if the pool was opened. Mattie nodded.

"I'm going upstairs Mattie and get into my swimsuit. It will be good to get in the pool again."

MaryRose was floating on her back, enjoying herself immensely, when she heard her mother calling. She swam to the edge of the pool at the same time her Mother walked to the edge. She jumped out of the pool and quickly dried herself to give her mom a big hug, "Mom, it is so good to see you."

"And you MaryRose, but why didn't you let us know you were coming home. I spoke to Auntie Marge two days ago and she said nothing about you leaving the convent. No matter, I'm just so happy to have you here."

"Mom, we have so much to talk about and we have plenty of time to do it. On the ride home from the convent, I did a lot of thinking mostly about what I want to do for the next six months."

"I didn't know you had a time frame to do anything. Tell me about your plans." As Mair started to talk, she saw Mattie coming down the path with a tray of ice tea. Mair jumped up and took the tray from Mattie and said, "Come sit with us Mattie. This tea is just what we need." It wasn't until quite late that night that Mair and her Mother were able to sit alone to have their chat.

They were sitting on the sun porch out back on a beautiful summer's night. They hadn't been there long when her Dad joined them. "Am I allowed to join you two ladies?"

"Of course Dad, I just wanted to let you guys know what my tentative plans are for the next six months.

"Why for only six months? Do you make plans every six months at a time?"

"Not every six months Dad, just for the next six months. I think I had told you I wanted to take a year off to do a lot of thinking and try to find out exactly what I wanted to do the rest of my life. I was here for a while and then I spent a great deal of time with Auntie Marge, which was time well spent. I have about six months left and what I'm hoping to do is to go to a place like Haiti, where I can help other people. I've done so much for myself in going to college, going to England and Harvard, but all that was for me."

"You think doing a good deed is going to help you find yourself, to find what you want to spend the rest of your life doing?" Her Dad was quite taken back and puzzled how going to a place like Haiti was going to help decide her lifework. The three talked well into the night and more than likely nothing definitive was really accomplished.

"Mom and Dad don't think for one minute I'm going to throw away my education. I love the law, particularly international law and I want it to be very much part of my life. What I need to know is what path I'm going to embrace to use that knowledge. To be clearer, am I going to be part of a law firm, do just research work do church law, or perhaps enter the convent and practice law where I can for them. I jump from one idea to the next and I don't come up with any definitive answers and I feel maybe I need a completely different atmosphere, completely foreign to what I'm used to. Do you understand? You both have given me everything I ever needed, and now I have to give myself what I need and I have to find myself.

Her father thought a moment before he said, "You do make a lot of good sense MaryRose, but there is one thing you haven't mentioned, and that's love and marriage. Does that enter into your life?"

Before Mair could answer her father, they all heard "Mom, Mom, Dad," it was Chuck screaming. The three adults jumped up and ran towards the kitchen. "Mom, Mom, Dad, look at Mattie I think something's wrong, I tried to wake her but she doesn't move." Everyone rushed to Mattie and MaryRose got down on her knees and rubbed her arms that were lying across the table with her head resting on top of one arm. Mair stood up immediately and said to call 911 right away. The emergency truck arrived about ten minutes later. The paramedics checked her vital signs and prepared to put her on the stretcher.

Bill Gillian took aside one of the paramedics and gave him the pertinent information needed. One question he couldn't answer was how old Mattie was. Everybody kind of looked at each other, wondering how old is Mattie? Marianne truly had to think and realize she really didn't know her age and started to figure how old Mair was when she first started working for them. "I'm not exactly sure. I believe she's in her early sixties. She has some papers in a desk in her room and I'll look through them and bring the information to the hospital."

Mair followed the ambulance to Arlington hospital. Her Mom, Dad and Chuck arrived shortly after. Fortunately the emergency rooms were not full probably because of the very late hour, so Mattie was taken care of immediately. The family on the other hand, paced back and forth waiting to get information on Mattie's condition. Finally the doctor came to the waiting room and told the family that Mattie had a heart attack. "It doesn't appear to be a major heart attack, but a heart attack nonetheless. No matter how slight or serious it has to be carefully dealt with. I'm going to send her to intensive care more of a precaution, but I want to see what her condition is in the morning and then we'll have a better idea what her situation is."

It was a nearly dawn before the family got to bed. Marianne was so thankful that Lyn had spent the night at her friend's house. It would've been a difficult scene for her to witness. No one slept very long and Mair was the first one of the family to come down to the kitchen. Mair made it big pot of coffee and one by one the family struggled to wake up and strolled into the kitchen. The doctor had told them before they left the hospital last night he would call them in the morning to tell them of Mattie's condition. Everyone tried to busy themselves to ease the wait. Marianne called Mrs. Hopkins to ask her to keep Lyn for the afternoon, and when hearing about Mattie she was only too happy to do so. Bill and Chuck called their respective offices to say they would be late for work. Then they all sat and waited. The call from the doctor finally came about noontime. There was complete silence in the room while Bill listened to the Doctor's report. Everyone knew that it was good news, as soon as there was a broad smile on Bill's face.

"Mattie is going to be all right. It was a mild heart attack and they are going to keep her in the hospital a few days to monitor her condition. They have taken her to the second floor and she can have visitors later on this afternoon," Bill gladly reported the information to his family.

"And now my dear family," Chuck stood up and said, "I do have some news that I think you all should know and before anybody interrupts me. Christine and I have set a wedding date."

"That is great news son, and when is this momentous occasion happening?"

"February twenty-eighth of next year."

"That is fantastic news," Mair said, "wait till Mattie hears this, she'll be thrilled to pieces. I think I'll run to the hospital to see Mattie now, but Chuck I won't say a word; that's for you to do."

CHAPTER TEN

Mattie came home from the hospital five days after her mild heart attack. It was the family's consensus Mattie would no longer do all the housework and the million other things she did every day to take care of the Gillian family and household. She always loved to cook and she was a great cook, so it was decided to let her continue. However, Marianne Gillian hired a cleaning woman to come in twice a week. At first Mattie did not agree, but soon realized she wasn't as strong and did tire easily. She conceded as long as when she was stronger Marianne would agree to let whoever leave.

MaryRose's father had several long talks with his daughter, mainly to get some insight into her thinking. He felt somehow, somewhere along the line, he lost touch with Mair's thinking. He felt it was most likely because she was away at school for so long, and basically out of touch, so now was the time to get caught up. On one of these conversations both he and MaryRose talked about her getting a place of our own. She thought this was a good idea, and had been thinking about it ever since their talk, but on the other hand, did nothing to make it a reality. And then she got a phone call from her Notre Dame roommate, Jenna. It had been some time since the two girls talked, so they had much to discuss. Before the conversation ended Jenna asked,

"Mair, why don't you come out and visit us. We have the room and we would love to see you." Like a bolt of lightning, Mair immediately knew this was what she should do. She told Jenna that she would get back to her in the next day or two and make definite plans.

She told her parents at the dinner table about her plans to go see Jenna. They all agreed it would be a great idea. After dinner Mair helped clear the table and brought the dishes into the kitchen. Mattie followed her with the remainder of the dishes. The Gillian women have been taking turns washing the dinner dishes.

"Mattie, go sit out on the sun porch with the folks, I can get these dishes done."

"I'll go out in a minute Mair, but I have something on my mind and it's been bothering me so I want to talk to you for a minute."

"Sure Mattie. Is something wrong?"

"No, while you were away visiting Auntie Marge a phone call came for you, which I answered. It was that young man, Phil I've heard you talk about. I know you told us all if this Phil should call here, not to tell him where you were, which I didn't. When you came home, you never asked if he called so I never mentioned it, and then I forgot about it. The other day, I remembered about the call and it bothered me that I never even told you."

"Mattie, don't you worry, it's perfectly all right," Mair said and hesitated a moment, "but I'm glad you did tell me now."

Mair had a hard time getting to sleep that night. It had been some time since she even heard Phil's name and hearing it now brought a flood of memories. She fought with herself over the idea if she should or should not call him. She finally dropped off to sleep and the next morning she immediately made reservations to Arkansas and called Jenna to tell her she was leaving in two days.

When MaryRose got off the plane Jenna, Stan and their three children where there to meet her. It was a wonderful reunion. Mair knew about little five-year-old Maria and three-year-old Mike, but one-year-old Jenny was a surprise. Jenna and Stan had a beautiful sprawling ranch home in the upscale suburbs of Little Rock, Arkansas.

Stan was a successful realtor and they just started a construction company. After a delicious dinner Stan did the dishes while Jenna and Mair got the children ready for bed. Mair was in charge of the baby, but had never even held a baby before, let alone change her diaper. Nonetheless with Jenna's guidance, she got an A+ according to the Mommy. Mair was amazed it really didn't take long before all three children were settled for the night. The two women talked until three a.m. getting caught up on each other's lives. The next five days were the happiest ever but seeing Jenna and Stan lives so complete, so stable and so loving left Mair feeling empty. Baby Jenny was a prize, but Mikey and Marie stole Mair's heart away. They became her buddies for life. Mair had five wonderful days but her plane was leaving for home the next day. Both Jenna and Stan urged her to stay longer, but for the first time MaryRose knew what she would do next.

It was a few weeks now before Chuck's and Christine's wedding, so it was a hectic time around the Gillian home. Mair and Lyn are bridesmaids and both are giving a shower for Christine this coming Saturday. The bridesmaids had picked out their gowns before the Christmas holidays, which are a beautiful shade of blue. Marianne's and Mattie's dresses are a pretty shade of light lavender. Now that the shower is over all the Gillian girls are all set for the wedding.

The wedding took place at the cathedral in Arlington and it was the social event of the winter. No one could match the beauty of the bride, or the very handsome groom.

The reception took place in a large Arlington hotel and it too was a grand affair. It was nice to see so many young people there. As Mattie said, "I think there is every boy who has been in our house here tonight." Chuck and Christine left the reception for their honeymoon around eleven PM and the remaining Gilliam's left at midnight. It took a full week to get back to normal at the Gillian household.

With the whirlwind wedding festivities over, the Gillian family finally got back to their routine. Mair now knew what she was going to do. As she always did she was very direct and to the point. "I wanted you all to know that I finally made up my mind to enter the convent at the Sisters of the Angels." MaryRose sat down with her mother and Father and Mattie to tell them her decision. Noting her family's reaction and seeing no one fainted continued, "As you know I have thought of this for a long time, and until recently I wasn't sure if this was right for me, but now I really do feel it is right."

"Well, I for one am surprised," her father blurted out, "I have heard this from you before, but you always backed out for one reason or another. I have no idea what your reasoning was then. However, you've had many life experiences, so I expect this time there will be no backing out. Let me say this; if this is your calling I am delighted and you know that all of us sitting here are one hundred percent behind you."

MaryRose listened intently to her father and she realized that she was letting her emotions show as tears rolled down her cheeks. She wiped them away and simply said, "I love you, Dad. Thank you."

Mattie got up from her chair and went over to MaryRose and kissed her and said, "God bless you, my child." MaryRose could tell that her mother wasn't as positive as Mattie or her Dad. She just sat there with a little smile on her face, but also with a frown. MaryRose got up from her chair and went over to her Mother's chair and knelt before her.

"Mom, all I want from you is to be happy for me. I know I have been undecided for a long time, and in some ways, I haven't changed. I have prayed about this and I've come to the conclusion that God will be the one to decide if this is right for me. I treasure my education and I have that to thank you and Dad for and I intend to find a place in the order to use the gift of knowledge I've been given."

"MaryRose, believe me, I am happy for you and I do know God will direct you, I don't have to."

Then MaryRose called Father Paul and asked if he was free this afternoon, she would like to talk to him. "By all means, do come. I really didn't get a chance to talk to you for long at the wedding, so this will be a treat." Mair was anxious because Father Paul had always been her trusted counselor. They talked for over an hour about MaryRose's decision and like her parents Father Paul had heard her desire many times before and deep down he always thought she did have a vocation. All in all, he was happy for her. Before she left to go home, they both went into the church and prayed together.

As soon as Mair got home, she called the Sisters of the Angels and their Mother Superior, Auntie Marge, to ask if she would accept her as a novitiate at her convent. Her aunt didn't say yes or no; rather she said to be there in two weeks.

In her preparation Mair really didn't know what was appropriate to bring with her. So she made another quick call to Auntie Marge and was told, "Just bring yourself and your dowry my dear. Your needs will be provided."

A month later, Sister MaryRose was a novice of the Sisters of the Angels. Her long hair cut short, covered by a white short white material held on by a head band and dressed all in white just like six other girls. She ate, prayed, went to classes, and even sung vespers (she feared she might be kicked out of the order once they heard her voice), scrubbed floors, cleaned bathrooms, washed and ironed clothes, as all the other novices did too. Like everything this young woman accomplished, she devoted her time and energy to the convent and did everything well, (except singing). One time, she asked Mother Superior to give her singing lessons. Her answer was "God loves your voice; use it".

Each sister had a conference once a month with Mother Superior to talk about any issues that may be bothering them or any problems needing attention, physical or mental. It was time for Sister MaryRose to go for her monthly meeting. It was difficult for both women to forget they were related. However, Mother Superior did well in this regard, but Mair had difficulty separating the two.

"Good afternoon aunt - excuse me - Mother Superior." Mair said as she was called into the office. "I will honestly try to keep the proper protocol Mother Superior."

"It's hard to believe MaryRose this is the end of six months at the convent, time has gone by so fast. In some ways you have come to a turning point. Now it is time to consider what commitments you will make in the near future. Observing you, and in some ways you seem to be distancing yourself from the other sisters. Is there some problem there?"

"No," Sister MaryRose paused and then, "I don't believe so. Oh, I guess I do find our age difference a sticky point. Some girls are as much is ten years younger and that is quite a spread at their age."

"Do you mean their lack of maturity?"

"Yes I suppose so," MaryRose answered.

"Did you ever think to enlighten and encourage these girls to show them what maturity is?"

"I'm not sure I know what you mean."

"MaryRose you are a well-educated woman and some of these girls barely got out of the eighth grade. Use your education to show and teach them. Think about it, MaryRose with some understanding you can do a lot for these girls. You can help them to mature by your example."

MaryRose stood there with her head hanging down. This is all new to her; she had never been reprimanded before. The Mother Superior walked towards her and with her finger lifted her head. "Sister MaryRose I watched you doing your garden work, which looks just beautiful, but you're always alone. Take one of the girls and teach them what you do so they can do the same thing," the nun smiled and returned to her desk. "It is important for you to start thinking seriously about the commitments you are about to make in a few short months."

"Yes, Mother, I will."

After MaryRose left the office, Mother Superior knew in her heart, her niece was on the edge. The conference at the end of MaryRose's seventh month, as well as the eighth month went much smoother and MaryRose seemed to be much more confident in her convent role. Then in the middle of the critical ninth month and the taking of their first vows the Mother Superior received a phone call from her sister, Marianne. "How are you doing Marge? I know I promised you I would not call during MaryRose's novice months, but I have very sad news, which I will leave up to you as to how and what to tell MaryRose."

"My heavens Marianne, what has happened?"

"Our dear friend, Mattie had a major heart attack two nights ago. We took her immediately to the hospital where she was placed in intensive care, and we had high hopes that she would survive however, Mattie died this afternoon," Marianne said between her sobs. "Marge as you know, she was such a dear person and probably the best friend I had or will ever have again. I had no choice except to call you, and as I said, I trust you to do the right thing in telling MaryRose. She loved her dearly and this will be a great loss to her also."

"I'm so sorry to hear this Marianne and I promise you I will be as gentle as possible telling MaryRose. Call me when the funeral arrangements are made. God bless you and the entire family, I know this is a tremendous loss."

The Mother Superior knew she had a difficult task ahead. She felt for some time now, MaryRose was teetering on the edge of her vocation and this news would either make or break that edge. She asked God to guide her words in telling MaryRose this sad news. She called Sister Joel to find out where Sister MaryRose was and when she returned, she said, "Sister MaryRose is in the garden. Shall I tell her to come to the office?' The nun shook her head and decided the garden would probably be the best place to tell her niece this sad news..

It was a beautiful late spring day and the sky was a spotless azure. As the Mother Superior strolled through the garden, she couldn't help but notice the beautiful gardens which she knew were planted by Sister MaryRose. A short distance down the path she found her niece on her hands and knees planting periwinkles. She called, "Sister, you have done a beautiful job here. I don't believe the gardens ever look so beautiful. Come and sit with me on the bench over there."

"Oh, Mother, I am so dirty."

"No matter, here take my hanky and just wipe off your hands." MaryRose did as she was told and sat next to Mother Superior. Her aunt took her niece's hand in hers and said, "I am so sorry I have sad news to tell you, MaryRose."

"Oh my God, something happened to my mother, dad, the kids?"

"No, my child, Mattie died of a heart attack last night," Auntie Marge, slowly said.

A look of shock crossed MaryRose's face and she cried, "No – oh no, Auntie Marge I must go, I must go home. I just can't believe it; she was doing so well," she cried as the tears flowed easily down her cheek.

"Your mother is going to call and let us know what the funeral arrangements are." her aunt said, as she cradled her niece in her arms.

"No, no, Auntie Marge, I must go now, I must be there for my parents, but most of all to be there for my dear Mattie."

"Sister MaryRose I want you to take a deep breath and try to relax a bit. They're just as important things here that we must talk about. You have made a commitment to God and yourself. At this point in time MaryRose, I cannot let you go home. You have three more weeks until you take your vows and during those three weeks' time here is intense and important to your vocation. Do you understand what I'm telling you?"

All while the Mother Superior spoke, MaryRose was shaking her head, and finally, she said, "Auntie Marge, I have to follow my heart and my heart is aching to be with my family and take part in Mattie's burial. The urge to be there is stronger than anything I've ever felt. Give me your blessing to leave now to do what I feel I must do."

"I want you to go into the Chapel and ask God for his help and think logically of what the consequence is because of what you're doing. Remember my dear, Mattie is with God, she has reached her ultimate goal and happiness and she would not want you to in anyway change your course in life for her. So go to the chapel and find out what God wants you to do.

MaryRose did go to the chapel and sat in the first pew. She didn't say a word, just sat there thinking about all the years Mattie took care of her and how in reality she was her mother. She thought how her parents were gone most every day, but Mattie was always there for her. And then there was Chuck two years later, and even seven years later when Charlyn was born, Mattie was there for them too. We were her family who she loved and cared for each and every day. She told God that she was painfully confused and begged Him to show her the way. She sat there for another half hour, just sitting, thinking and crying.

Finally she left the chapel and went to the general sitting room, and put a collect phone call to Chuck's house, and she was glad he answered the phone. "Chuck it's me - Mair, could you please come up to the convent and pick me up?"

"Sure, what's up," Chuck asked.

"I don't want to call Mom and Dad to come and get me. God knows they have enough to do with getting Mattie - well you know all they have to do, so I thought if you could come pick me up, I'd be so grateful."

"Yeah sure. When do you want me to come?" Chuck said, still sounding a bit confused.

"As soon as possible, please." and Chuck could tell she started to cry.

"Okay, I'll leave right away - is that what you want me to do?"

"That would be great. It will take you about forty-five minutes to get here and I'll wait for you at the gate, you remember the gate to the garden?"

"Yeah, I think so. Christine will come with me; she was up there once with you and Mom, right?"

"Yes - yes, she was. I'll be waiting for you at the gate. Thanks, Chuck it means so much to me."

113

MaryRose sat at the small desk in her room and wrote a note to Mother Superior. She knew this wasn't the proper way to do things, but she couldn't face her aunt again. She felt her head was going to explode. She put the note in an envelope, and then gathered up the very few personal things she had. She knew this was the time of day when the other girls, with Mother Superior and Sister Joel, would be in Bible study. She looked at the small clock on the desk, telling her Chuck should be there in ten to fifteen minutes. She quietly slipped through the halls, stopped at the chapel, and walked to the garden door. She immediately rushed down the garden path to the gate, opened it and went out. It wasn't that long, although it seemed forever to Mair, when Chuck's car pulled up to the curb. She quickly opened the back car door, got inside and told Chuck to drive off. Christine immediately asked, "Are you all right, MaryRose?"

"Yes I am and I can't thank you both enough. I just had to get home and rather than cause an uproar at the convent, I chose the chicken way out, which I'm sure I'm going to regret but to tell you the truth, at the moment I didn't feel I had a choice. Now tell me how are Mom and Dad?"

"They can't wait to see you Mair. I didn't know if you wanted me to call them or tell them you were coming home. Nevertheless I called Mom, shortly before we left," Chuck confessed.

"Of course, that's fine. I'm sure it seems so, but I'm not trying to hide anything from anybody. I thought if I let Mom know ahead of time, she might call Auntie Marge and I just wanted to leave the convent without an emotional scene. I must make it clear; Auntie Marge was absolutely wonderful to me and all the girls that are at the convent. She is a very, very special woman and I'm glad she's part of our lives...I know I'll have to hang my head low and apologize for this.

Chuck wasn't sure where MaryRose wanted to go, to his house or home. When he asked her at first she didn't answer, but finally said home. Before Chuck and Christine left to pick MaryRose up at the convent he did call his Mother and found out that she had already spoken to Auntie Marge and knew she would be on her way home. He couldn't help wonder if Auntie Marge told her how terrible MaryRose felt. Certainly neither Christine nor Chuck had ever seen her look so bad. Chuck was very concerned. During the forty-five minute trip MaryRose didn't say a word.

When they got to the family home, Mair insisted she go in the house alone. She unlocked the kitchen door, opened it slowly and this overwhelming feeling of loss consumed her as she entered the kitchen. She had no idea where her parents were and tried very hard to pull herself together for when they did arrive. In the meantime, Chuck called his mom on her cell phone to alert her of MaryRose's condition.

"I just left the church with Father Paul; we were making the final arrangements for the funeral. "What do you mean, Mair is so bad? Auntie Marge told me she was very concerned."

"Mom, I don't mean to sound alarming, but I just wanted you to be aware. When is Dad getting home?"

"He should be on his way home now. Thanks honey and again thank you for getting your sister."

Marianne parked her car and rushed into the kitchen. Mair was sitting at the kitchen table and she almost looked like she was in a trance. Her Mother went over and put her arms around her daughter and then Mair looked up at her. She looked down at her daughter and was shocked. She too, had never seen Mair look so bad. "MaryRose, I bet you haven't had anything to eat. Let me fix you something, or at least a hot cup of tea; she didn't wait for an answer and put the kettle on the stove. Minutes later she sat down across the table from Mair, took her hands in her own and simply said, "I love you." MaryRose smiled and said nothing.

After Mair had taken a few sips of the tea, she got up and said, "Mom, if you don't mind, I'm really exhausted. I think I'll go to my room, take a shower, and lay down for a while. Is that all right with you?"

About a half-hour or so later Bill came home. Marianne met him at the door and said, "Bill I am so glad you're home. I've never seen MaryRose in this condition, and I'm worried."

"Chuck called me, but before he did Marge called me from the convent. They both filled me in of what's going on with Mair. I thought about it since I left the office. I know MaryRose was very fond of Mattie. We all were very fond of Mattie. She was a part of all of our lives for many, many years. I know Mair is grieving, but I believe there's something more here."

"I don't understand what you mean Bill?"
"Marianne our daughter is a very strong woman, and yes, Mattie's death was a shock and a loss to us all. We know as well as MaryRose knows, life goes on. My Lord Mattie had a wonderful life and had nothing to regret. I think this news didn't help her struggling."

"Her struggling? What does MaryRose have to struggle about?"

"Hear me out dear. I believe MaryRose has done the unconscionable thing - she failed. She was so sure that she had a vocation. She wanted the vocation so much she thought, but in reality she found out she didn't. She failed her Auntie Marge, she failed us, when in reality she only failed herself. Let's face it, MaryRose has never failed in anything and she doesn't know how to handle failure. Marge agreed with me, Marianne."

"You both are probably right, but how does MaryRose realize this?"

"I think the one to handle it is probably Father Paul. Do you agree?' His wife went to him and he held her close, and said, "I really think darling, that this is a little stone in the road, a little setback for MaryRose, but you know Marianne, it might be the best thing that ever happened. She will realize you don't have to be perfect all the time.

Bill called Father Paul and gave him a little synopsis of what was going on and they both decided that since the funeral was tomorrow it would be better to have MaryRose come to the rectory the following morning at Father Paul's request.

The sun shone brightly, just the way Mattie liked it. She would take it as a beautiful day to go to heaven. There wasn't a vacant seat in the church, in fact standing room only. How appropriate! Father Paul gave a wonderful homily telling the congregation of all the little things Mattie did that no one knew about. He said she should be an inspiration to us all. Father Paul himself said she probably was the kindest person he ever knew. There wasn't a dry eye in the church, but there might be tears, but the smiles were bigger.

As the mourners were exiting the church after Mass, Father Paul took MaryRose aside and asked her to come see him tomorrow morning.

CHAPTER ELEVEN

MaryRose was anxious to see Father Paul the morning after Mattie's funeral. She took a shower, dressed and went down to the kitchen for breakfast. There was no one in the kitchen and Mair felt like a lost child without Mattie there to tell her good morning. She wondered how people get over the loss of a dear one, because she couldn't imagine life in the Gillian household without Mattie. She knows everyone says, "it takes time," but how do you stop missing someone you loved?

When she arrived at Father Paul's rectory she had to smile at the rectory-trailer. Her dad had told her the parish wanted to build him a real building for his rectory, but Father Paul absolutely refused. She knocked on his door, but heard him calling her from the church. She turned and waved, walking to meet him. He greeted her and then said, "Remember years ago Mair, how we would have all our discussions in the back row of the church? I thought this discussion should be there too." Mair smiled and the two went into the back row of the church. After a short time of small chatter, Father finally said; "Mair, why did you leave the convent?"

"Why? To come home to Mattie's funeral, of course."

"Of course," the priest said, "you left to come home, but you also left the convent. You left your vocation." MaryRose never thought of it that way, and it took her a few minutes to reply.

"I guess I've disappointed a lot of people."

"No, no. MaryRose you disappointed yourself, no one else. They sat in the back of the church for about an hour. Father Paul desperately trying to convince MaryRose her leaving the vocation had nothing to do with Mattie's death. Her leaving the convent and her vocation was because deep down she found, in fact, she didn't have a true vocation. Mair tried to argue the fact, but Father Paul would have none of it.

Father walked Mair to her car and said, "Mair, there is no shame in realizing one makes a mistake. God has other plans for you, my dear woman and He'll show you in His own time." There were tears in her eyes and she thanked the priest, telling him in her heart, she knew he was right.

"One thing Mair, I'm being transferred and it's with regret I have to leave Saint Anne's, but like you I have to move on. I'm being transferred to a small parish in West Virginia named Saint Matthew, so if you are ever around the area be sure to stop by and say hello." She gave the man a hug with tears in her eyes.

As Mair got in the car, she turned and said, "I'll see you again, and that's a promise." And she drove off. While driving she thought how right Father was in telling her there'll always be changes in our life and we have to accept them and move on.

Again, she came home to an empty house. Mom and Dad were at work, Chuck doesn't live here anymore and her sister Lyn was at soccer practice. Yes indeed life does have many changes. She telephoned the Sisters of Angels convent to speak to Auntie Marge. Sister Joel asked MaryRose to wait a minute, and shortly Auntie Marge said, "Oh my dear

MaryRose; I am so glad to hear from you." The nun could tell immediately from the tone of her niece's voice everything is all right. The nun had kept in close touch with her sister so she knew MaryRose was slowly finding herself. MaryRose started to apologize to her, and she shook her head, "You don't owe me an apology and I want you to know I'm not disappointed in you in any shape or form. I know whatever the future brings, you will be a happy, successful person and that's all I want for you. I might add, that's all God wants for you too, that is if – you keep in touch with me." Both women laughed.

Lyn came barging in the back door and immediately went to the refrigerator, then said, "Mair whose cooking dinner?"

"We are. I did a little cooking in college you know. I bet the two of us could come up with a good meal." And they did. There were just about finished when their mother came in carrying some take- out food. It was decided the take-out would be good for tomorrow and asked their Mom to set the table – they all laughed at that. Dinner was ready by the time Dad came home. The dinner of stuffed green peppers was quite good, which they all enjoyed to the amazement of everybody. Dinner finished, Mair started to clear the table. When she came back to the table to collect some more dishes, she sat down at the table instead.

"Okay, fellow Gillian's I think since there are only three women in this house we have to set up a schedule. So the bulk of the work isn't upon just one." After all three women had something to say, pro and con, the master of the house, Mr. Gillian tapped his glass for silence.

"Since I am the judge and jury in this house, I strongly suggest every night we're at home for dinner, one lady will prepare the dinner, set the table, clear the table, and do the dishes…" Before he could finish, there was an uproar amongst the ladies and they unanimously voted the man of the house down. They finally decided it was the duty of everyone to do his share, especially good old Dad.

"Before everyone leaves and with all our culinary duties finished, I forgot to mention Father Paul is going to be transferred to a parish in West Virginia. He didn't say when he was leaving, but I'm sure it's not in the too distant future. He is one who's going to be sorely missed in this town." The doorbell rang and Lyn rushed to answer to let her friends in who came to play tennis. To Mair's surprise, two boys and another girl came in the kitchen so Lyn could introduce them to her big sister. Introductions over, the foursome left for the tennis court. Mom and Dad went out on the sun porch to relax and all of a sudden MaryRose felt left. She thought everyone else has something to do, some place to go, someone to talk to, and here she stood alone. She decided right then and there it was time for her to move on. She went into the sun porch sat down with her parents and said, "As you both know I saw Father Paul this morning and I think he straightened out my thinking or better said my lack of thinking, but one thing is for sure, it's time for me to look ahead and not backwards. So, I'm going to get a job in downtown DC.

"A job? What kind of a job? her Father asked.

Some time ago I was in downtown Washington, shopping I guess, whatever, I noticed a storefront law office. I went in and there was a secretary or a receptionist at a desk in front, and down the Hall on each side were offices, which I presume were for two lawyers. I chatted with the young lady for a few minutes asking general questions!

"What is the name of the practice?"

"Dad, I'm not really sure, I think it might be Clarkson – maybe Clarkson and Son. But what I want to say is I think I'd like to apply for the job there."

"MaryRose you know you can have a job in any law firm. What I don't understand is why this little under distinguished office?"

"I can't answer that Dad, but I think it might be because it's obviously a new firm and just maybe I can give them the boost it needs. Do you think I'm being too presumptuous?"

"No, not really, MaryRose. If you had to start at the bottom of the ladder like most law graduates do, it would be more understandable. You aren't at the bottom of the ladder and you could get any job you applied for."

"That's just it Dad. I think it's time I did start at the bottom and perhaps I would have a much better understanding of where I belong, of what my calling truly is, instead of jumping all over the place and winding up with nothing."

"You may be right, but on the other hand, you may have a problem with the Gillian name. As you know, it's a very prominent name, a name which I'm sure this law office you're talking about, knows."

"I thought about that too, and do I tell them that I am the Gillian of the most famous law firm in DC, or tell them there are a lot of other Gillian's? I'm sure Dad, I couldn't do that as long as they know I'm not there to take over, or I'm not using them as a stepping stone to your office. Dad, what I'm trying to say, I don't want them, nor do I feel, I'm trying to use them in any way for an ulterior motive."

"MaryRose, you know Dad and I have the utmost faith in you. Whatever you do with your life, we are one hundred percent behind you."

"I know Mom and I want you both to know I treasure your opinions and I take them to heart, but at this point in my life I have to do what you taught me to believe."

Monday morning, MaryRose showered and dressed in smart sleeveless sheath with a waist length jacket. She looked in her mirror and hardly recognized herself; it had been a long time since she wore anything that even resembled the smart looking outfit. She had a quick bite to eat, looked at the time and decided most of the rush hour should be over, so she got in her car and headed for downtown DC. When she reached her destination, the next problem was to find a place to park. She finally found a parking garage a few blocks away and was thankful there was space or two left. She walked back to the law office and looked at the sign above the door. It read; Gerald Clarkson – Attorney. Well I wasn't too far off, she thought.

She entered and walked to the receptionist's desk and introduced herself and said she was looking for a position. The young woman told MaryRose she wasn't aware there was a position open at this time, but if she would like to fill out an application she would put it on file. MaryRose filled it out and brought it back to the receptionist's desk. The lady looked it over and turned to MaryRose and asked her if she could wait a moment or two. MaryRose knew her application was impressive and just the fact that she was asking for a position as a graduate of Harvard Law was enough to catch an eye. MaryRose took her seat again and waited. Maybe it was ten minutes later when the young lady came out of the law office, accompanied by a gentleman who now held the application in his hand.

He walked directly to where MaryRose was sitting. She stood and he said, "How do you do Miss Gillian, I am Gerry Clarkson. It's a pleasure to meet you. If you don't mind, would you come back to my office? There are several things I'd like to go over with you." She followed him to his office and he asked her to sit in a chair in front of his desk. He was continually looking at her application and finally said, "Am I correct you are here to apply for a position?"

"That is correct. Is there something wrong?"

"Not at all, as far as your application goes, not at all. May I ask, are you Tucker Gillian's daughter? And if so, why are you applying for a job here?"

"Yes I am Tucker Gillian's daughter. I understand your questioning however I did not choose to work in my Father's law firm."

"May I ask why?" Mr. Clarkson was obviously confused.

"Sir, my Father didn't start out where he is now, plus the fact I studied international law and research and my Father's law firm has nothing to do with my studies."

"Miss Gillian, our firm is primarily real estate law."

"Yes sir, I know, but certainly, I would think - correct me if I'm wrong - there is a lot of research to do in real estate law. If so I would find that very interesting," MaryRose remarked.

"The name Gillian is well known in DC and surrounding areas. If you were to work here that could be a boost to our business...to that, there's no doubt. My partner, Fred Hilton isn't in the office, however I will see him later and discuss your application. I will call you in the morning. They both stood and he escorted her to the door. If he said thank you for coming once, he said it three or four times. MaryRose thanked him and said she looked forward to his call in the morning.

Since she had a parking place, MaryRose decided to go to the fashionable clothier where her sister-in-law, Christine worked, and hoped she had time to have lunch with her. It was a little walk away, but MaryRose enjoyed the beautiful day as well as walking; she hadn't done that in some time. Mair was glad she made the decision to see Christine because it was the first time the two had a one on one conversation. She found Chuck's wife witty, intelligent and very much in love with her brother.

The awaited call from Gerald Clarkson came one minute after nine the next morning. There was no doubt MaryRose had the job. He asked when it would be convenient for her to come to the office to set up her time, salary and her expectations. He also was anxious for her to meet his partner, Fred Hilton. It was agreed upon Monday of the next week.

Mair spent the next five days shopping for the appropriate work wardrobe, which just about depleted her trust fund left to her by her grandparents. She also had her auburn hair cut and styled along with a new manicure. It was amazing how the feeling of self-worth came over her. At ten a.m. Monday morning, MaryRose entered the building of Gerald Clarkson law offices. She immediately noticed a new desk and chair was placed perpendicular to the receptionist's desk. She went over to the receptionist and said, "I'm sorry, but I never did get your name and since we're about to be desk-mates I'd like to know yours. My name is MaryRose.

The young woman stood and came around to her desk and said, "I'm so glad to meet you. I am Susan Clarkson."

"Are you, Mr. Clarkson's wife?"

Susan laughed and said, "no – no, I'm his sister." Then MaryRose joined her laughter. The two lawyers came out of their offices and Gerry introduced Fred Hilton to MaryRose and then told her she was welcome to change her desk in any way she wanted. He also told her she would find applications which Susan placed in her desk drawers; these would help her investigating different avenues of Real Estate. All in all, MaryRose felt very comfortable and at ease in her new job.

The four office mates, as they called themselves, soon fell into a workable routine. MaryRose's hours were from ten-thirty a.m. until five-thirty p.m., presumably because of the early a.m. traffic and parking problems, or more realistic – payroll problems. Susan arrived earlier in the morning, but left around one o'clock or when MaryRose returned from lunch. Everyone seemed satisfied with the arrangement. MaryRose's name was painted on the front door window under the attorneys and below Gerry's and Fred's names. At least once a day someone came into the office and asked if Mair was part of the Tucker Gilliam law firm. It did break up the monotony.

The weeks turned into months and there was a notable increase in business, partially due to MaryRose and her efficiency in obtaining the needed permits, financial assistance, bank requirements, city ordinance information and so on. It wasn't long after both Gerry and Fred turned this part of the business completely over to MaryRose. By the way, her office mates almost always now called her Mair.

During a quiet time in the office, she was sitting at her desk reading a Real Estate pamphlet and happened to glance up and thought she saw Phil Kern walking by the office. Her heart skipped a beat as she got up and quickly went to the front door, walked out on the sidewalk and looked in the direction Phil had been walking, but he was nowhere in sight.

As soon as Mair returned to her desk she opened up her computer to find out where the FBI building was in regard to her office. To her surprise, it was only a few blocks south. There wasn't much work done that afternoon as Mair's mind was elsewhere. From that day forward, Mair tried to keep a close eye on the people passing by per chance one might be Phil. Weeks went by and still no Phil. Just as Mair was about to give up late one Friday afternoon, she was getting ready to leave the office and as she walked to the front door Phil passed as she walked out. "Phil – Phil" she called. He turned and looked back but didn't see her amongst the other walkers. She called again, "Phil – Phil

Kern." He saw her waving, turned, and looked unbelievably as he walked towards her. Mair stood frozen in her spot, but as soon as Phil got closer, she put out her arms to embrace him and he did the same to her.

"Mair I can't believe it's you...What are you doing down here? You don't look like a nun – are you still in the convent?"

"Phil, do you have a few minutes or longer? Perhaps we could go somewhere and have a drink or a cup of coffee. Whatever?"

He took her by the arm and said, "You bet we can, let's do it."

CHAPTER TWELVE

As it turned out Phil had his car in the same parking garage as Mair, so they climbed into the first one they came to which was Phil's. "Shall we go back to the 1879 club?" She nodded and in a few minutes, they were there. "Just can't believe that I'm seeing you." Phil said as he opened the car door for Mair.

"I know what you mean. I thought I saw you a couple weeks back, passing by the law office. When I went out you were lost in the crowd. I looked and looked but I couldn't find you. So when I saw you this evening, I didn't hesitate and called."

"And I'm very happy you did. Funny thing about it, I can count the times I parked the car in that parking garage. It must be fate," Phil said with a broad smile on his face. They were lucky to get a table in the restaurant as it was a Friday night. "Isn't this the same table we sat at a long time ago?" They ordered wine and their dinner and over coffee Phil asked, "Tell me how is Miss Mattie?"

MaryRose could not hide her surprise and said, "You knew Mattie?"

"No, I never met Mattie, but over the last year or so I talked to her on the phone. Actually, we became good friends. For a long time she would just say you weren't at home and she would give you a message if she heard from you. Every time I called, we got to chit chatting – you know how she was. She told me what she was doing and wanted to know what I was doing – that kind of stuff. Finally, she started telling me where you were, like she's in Arizona or she's in upstate Virginia, but never anything else. I asked her once why, she simply said because Mair told me not to."

"Phil, I'm sorry to have to tell you, Mattie died. I guess it is six months now. She had a major heart attack and died three days later." Phil reached across the table and held Mair's hand. It was obvious Mattie's death hurt her deeply. "She was really a dear friend. She literally brought up Chuck and Lyn as well as me. Mom and Dad were both working and we were babies, Lyn wasn't even born when she's first started taking care of us. She became a very important person to the entire family."

"I'm sure you all were just as important to her. We really became quite good phone friends and I always got the feeling she would've liked to tell me more, but never would betray your trust."

"Everybody loved her. She really was a very kind person - good to everybody. Mattie was never considered a housekeeper, or a maid, or even a babysitter; Mattie was family and was treated as such."

"And you told her not to tell me anything," Phil commented. "You're a meanie!"

"No just slightly insane." Mair laughed. They had a night-cap and then Mair asked Phil to take her to the car.

"I'll take you to your car Mair, but now that I've found you again, I'm not going to lose you. We will see each other again and again and again. Please don't run away from me because I need you, and more than that, I want you. I want you to be part of my life." Mair looked at him and started to say something but Phil put his finger to her mouth and said," Mair, please don't say anything. I'll call you in the morning." They drove to the parking garage pretty much in silence. Mair guided him to her car and he took the keys to unlock the driver's side door. With the door open, she turned towards him and he kissed her.

MaryRose was the first one down for breakfast. She put up the coffee and fixed herself some Rice Krispy and juice. Her Mom came in the kitchen while she was eating and said, "I didn't think you'd be up so early. After all it is Saturday."

"I know, but I couldn't sleep and I have several things I want to get done today. One of them is to look for an apartment, preferably on the Arlington side of the bridge. I really have no idea what's available anywhere. Have you heard of any great deals?" Her Mom left the room and came back with yesterday's paper and said she thought there would be many listings in Friday's paper.

"Thanks Mom. This will be a big help. As I said, I really don't know where to start."

"Well, if I hear of anything, I'll let you know. But you know darling, there is no rush. In fact, you never have to leave here."

"Mom, I really think at twenty-eight I should set up my own housekeeping, don't you think?"

"Of course MaryRose, and I understand completely. Speaking of changes, you know I went all through Mattie's belongings and in her desk I found an address book and it has the name of a cousin."

"You're kidding Mom. Did she ever mention to you she had a cousin? I never heard her talk about anybody or she had any family."

"I know Mair and the only reason why I know this is a cousin because in her address book, she put down: Cousin Martha with her phone number and a Virginia address. Well, anyway, I called the lady and come to find out she was at the funeral. She had read the obituary, but said she didn't want to interfere. We talked for quite a while and she sounded like a lovely lady I told her how fond we were of Mattie and how much we miss her. She really was part of our family. I asked her a couple questions like if she had a family or children, or did she work? She said no but she was looking for a new position and she too did housekeeping. Well needless to say she's coming over today and we're going to talk,"

"Mom, I think that's great. You really do need somebody here. I'm finding out it's not easy to work and to cook and keep house all in one day, plus taking care of children.

"Mair, the prime reason I'd like somebody here all the time is because of Lyn. You and Chuck had each other growing up and Lyn was so much younger. Anyway we'll see how things work out; she's to come this afternoon around three."

Mair was busy doing odds and ends, but if the truth be known she was waiting for Phil's telephone call. Suddenly, she decided *nuts to that*, and went upstairs to collect her things and then leave. "Mom, I'm going to run now, wish me luck. Hopefully I'll find something nice and affordable. I'll probably be back this afternoon; I'd like to meet Mattie's cousin. I'll try to get here around three. If not, I'll call." She was just about to get into her car when her Mom called from the doorway; she had a phone call. She wanted to tell her Mom to tell whoever was calling to call back later. She thought for a moment, trying not to be so indecisive, started her car and drove off. She was about two miles from the house and she called her Mother, "Mom was that Phil who called?"

"Yes, it was dear and he gave me his phone number and wants you to please call him" "Oh good, give me his number and I'll call later on," Mair answered trying to sound nonchalant.

She pulled to the side of the road and called Phil's number. After a couple rings, "Hey Mair I didn't think I'd hear so soon."

"I had to call my Mother shortly after I left. I forgot to ask her something and she told me you called and gave me your number and here I am. " (Honestly, MaryRose the Sisters at the convent would have your head telling such lies.) Mair thought.

"I wanted to know, Mair, if you haven't got any plans, could you come into the city for lunch?"

"Phil, I'm just on my way to Arlington. I want to look for an apartment closer to work and then I want to get back home by three o'clock to meet Mattie's cousin who is coming, and most likely Mom is going to hire her and come live with us."

"Are you free for dinner?"

"Yes, that may work."

"How about I come over there and pick you up. This way we don't have to work with two cars."

"I don't think I have to tell you where I live because I have a feeling you know darn well where I live, but that's great. How about six-thirty?"

"Sounds perfect Mair. I'll be anxious to find out how you made out apartment hunting. Good luck"

Before Mair restarted her car, she took out the newspaper and looked again at the real estate ads she had marked and decided her plan of attack.

It was almost three as MaryRose headed home. She was excited and couldn't wait to tell her parents about her new home. Most of the way she thought of how she could decorate the apartment to make it her own. As she drove in her driveway she noticed a strange car parked and thought it must be Mattie's cousin.

"Hi, where is everybody?" She called.

"We're in the living room. Come on in Mair," her Mother informed her. As MaryRose entered the room, her Mother said, "Dear, I'd like you to meet Mattie's cousin, Martha King." When introductions were over Mair excused herself. Realizing she was very hungry, she went into the kitchen and made herself a sandwich.

It was a good hour later her Mother went upstairs to Mair's bedroom. "What did you think of Martha; she seemed kind of nice," Mair asked.

"Yes I thought so too. The only problem is she's not too keen about staying here overnight. I told her to think about it, and I also wanted to talk to Dad. You know how often Dad has meetings and we have church things to attend at night. I suppose in a pinch we could work it out, but let's see what Dad has to say. I'm to call Martha tomorrow. But…did you find anything?"

"I did Mom, I'm so excited," I want you and Dad to come see it. I think you'll be pleased. Oh, and by the way, I signed a year lease."

"Well tell me where it is and all about this apartment."

"It's right off of Wisconsin – a few houses down. It is a basement apartment, but it only is three steps down as the upper house is several steps up. Anyway there are windows in the front, back and sides making it nice and bright. It has a good size kitchen and living room. There is a huge bathroom and a good size bedroom. And not only that – it's furnished and clean as can be. The landlord lives upstairs – Mr. and Mrs. Murphy. I guess they are about in their sixties and lovely people."

"It sounds perfect for you and close to everything including Georgetown so we can have lunch together now and then. I'm sure it's better than Arlington."

"Oh yes Mom. It's congested in the city and DC. All I could find were high-rises. No, I'm much better off where I'll be living."

"Wow, that was fast, but I guess working for real estate lawyers you knew exactly what to look for. I can't wait to see it."

"One more thing Mom. Phil is picking me up at six-thirty tonight. We're going out to dinner."

"Isn't he the FBI guy you can't stand?" her Mother questioned

"Yeah, he is."

"Well, if he is, I can't wait to meet him." And they both laughed. Later in the evening, MaryRose's parents and Lyn were eating dinner on the sun porch, when she came downstairs dressed for her date.

"Hi there, and don't you look lovely," her Dad greeted Mair as she kissed him on his forehead. "I have been hearing about your new little abode; it sounds perfect for what you need."

"I'm excited and I want you all to come and see it. I'm moving in a week from today," Mair said, just as the doorbell rang. Bill Gillian looked at his watch and it was six twenty-five.

"Aha. The guy is a prompt son of a gun. That's one point in his favor." Her father stated as Mair went to open the door

As soon as Phil saw her he said, "Wow, you look beautiful"

"Come meet the folks." He followed her into the sun porch and she said, "Dad, Mom and Lyn I want you all to meet Phil Kern," and then she turned to her father and said, "Dad, this is Philip." Introductions over Bill said, "Phil, how nice to meet you." And quickly, MaryRose joined in and said, "Dad, you guys have already eaten, but Phil and I haven't. I don't know about Phil, but I'm starved, so we're going to run.

"I hope I have the opportunity to talk to you another time, sir," Phil said. The two quickly left the room. As soon as Mair thought they were out of earshot she let Phil take her hand and he pulled her close to him, and asked, "Did I ever tell you?"

"Whatever tell me later." Mair answered. Once they got in the car, Mair started to tell him about her find of an apartment. She told him the whole layout and she would be moving in next Saturday.

"Terrific. That really sounds perfect for you. The only thing you didn't tell me where it is."

"Well, that's the greatest part of all because it's right around the corner off Wisconsin about a block down, which means I can walk to work."

"Which also means, I can walk to where you work and also to where you live," Phil remarked.

"Yeah, I've been wondering about that. The last time you passed by the office, I meant to ask you where you were coming from. I know the FBI building is down on Pennsylvania Avenue, and that's nowhere near my office."

Phil explained, "You're right, but I was coming from the field office over here at the Naval Security office. We have a field office on their grounds and every once in a while I have to check in there. They have several gates and one leads right out to Wisconsin." A few minutes later Mair told Phil to make the next right and park four or five houses down on the right. He parked along the curb and she pointed out this is where her new home is located. "Oh, I see what you mean; it's not really a basement apartment. It really doesn't look like there's any or at least not more than a foot underground. Can we go in and take a look?"

"I don't think so. It's almost dark and I don't want to disturb the Murphy's without notify them beforehand. We will have to work something out this week."

"Good enough. I'm excited for you," Phil said as he gave her a quick kiss.

They went to a small café in Georgetown and had a delightful dinner including a bottle of wine. The Café wasn't very crowded so they lingered over their coffee.

"Phil, you know an awful lot about me and I don't even know where you live in town. How about some info?"

"Well first of all, I'm not half as interesting as you are, so I don't want to bore you. I have a little house in Chevy Chase, but to tell you the truth I'm on the go so much I spend more time in hotel rooms then I do in my little house. I finally came to the conclusion it's time to sell it and get something here in the city."

"And when did you get involved with the FBI and why?" Mair wondered.

"After graduation from NYU, I spent three years in the Marine Corps and probably would've stayed in the Marines if I didn't get married. Susan wanted no part of service life. She was brought up in Maryland, so when I was discharged. Sue and I got married and settled near her parents in Maryland. As I told you we were only married a little over two years when she died. I thought then to go back in the service and one of my buddies was going down to Quantico, Virginia to train in the FBI. The idea interested me, so I went with him. And that my dear lady is my story in a nutshell."

"Are you happy in the FBI?"

"Yes, yes I am Mair. After all, I met you. We all do our bit in recruiting and it wasn't actually my forte until I met you. Now I'm into the investigating business and I love it."

"Really? I found investigating anything is very interesting and rewarding. I think working with Doctor Lee at Bristol was probably the most interesting adventure I had in the entire year I was in England. He taught me so much about what the power of good investigating accomplished."

"That's interesting," Phil said, "because that's exactly how I feel. Maybe you should think more about the FBI because when you come right down to it, that's what we're all about."

"I thought you were done recruiting?" Mair asked.

"Mair I don't think I'll ever stop recruiting you and I don't mean for the FBI. I think we should go home now and make mad passionate love." Mair sat across the table from him. She could feel the battle of her emotions within. They sat in silence for a couple of minutes until finally Phil said, "Perhaps for now I'd best take you home. However, I want you to know this isn't just the passion of the moment it's very real and I will wait until it's very real for you too." The two left the restaurant arm in arm and walked to his car. Phil opened the door for Mair and before she got in she put her arms around him and gave him a passionate kiss.

"Drive me across the bridge to my house. I'm not sure the time is right for us. Somehow I think the time might be coming, though. I think it's obvious to you, Phil, I do have feelings for you but I don't want them to be mixed up in the emotional mess in my head."

"Understood," is all Phil said. Mair got into the car and sat very close to him on the drive to her house. "I will call or stop by your office tomorrow morning. There's a possibility I might have to go to a field office in New York City. I won't know what the schedule is until I get into my office in the morning. All I want you to know and remember...I love you.

CHAPTER THIRTEEN

Phil did go to the field office in New York City and was going to be gone for about 18 or 19 days. He would keep in touch with Mair every time he had the opportunity. MaryRose on the other hand was kept busy making her apartment her home. Her mom and dad came to see the apartment and were delighted. They met the Murphy's who seemed happy to have MaryRose as a tenant. Her mother couldn't be more pleased having MaryRose's office and apartment so close to her work at Georgetown.

After the tour of their daughter's apartment, they went to the Shoreham Hotel and were served a delicious Sunday brunch. Mair asked her mom if she hired the new housekeeper Martha, hoping that was all taking care of. "No, Mair I didn't hire her and I'm not going to."

"Really Mom. I thought she was such a great idea."

"I thought so too, but while I was interviewing her several things popped up that made me uneasy.

"What was that?" Mair asked.

For one thing, she asked several times during our conversation how much Mattie had been paid. I told her Mattie got allowances, her room and board and for that matter, all her living expenses were paid for by us. Martha didn't seem to like that and told us she really didn't want to spend the nights at our house, but rather stay at home and receive a salary. Another thing she asked was what were her daily chores? Then the woman wanted to see Mattie's bedroom, which I told her it won't be necessary since she wasn't going to be using the room. I really became very uneasy.

"This was not another Mattie. I told her I would phone, after speaking to Mister Gillian."

"Wow, what a disappointment Mom. I'm glad you found her out before you hired her."

"I am too. I didn't even have to call her; Martha called us several times. She must've left a message on the machine three or four times. I finally did speak to the woman and told her I was sorry, but we had made other plans. I'll tell you, she was most indignant telling me we had wasted her time. However I do have good news. Father Paul sent over a lovely, lovely woman, Gracie. He told me she was a lot like Mattie and he was right. Lyn took to the woman right away and she starts with us tomorrow. Oh, before I forget, Auntie Marge called and said she wanted to hear from you."

"I feel bad Mom; I've been meaning to call her for a long time. I will call her as soon as we get home. Phil will still be out of town next weekend and if it works for Auntie Marge, I'll run out and see her then."

"Where is the man?" Her father asked. Mair proceeded to tell him Phil was working in New York. "Did you ever tell us what work Phil does?"

"Yeah, he is in the FBI."

"Right. Now all I remember he is the guy you hated." And everybody laughed.

MaryRose did call Auntie Marge who was very glad to hear from her. They made plans for Mair to spend the next weekend at the Sisters of the Angels convent. MaryRose no sooner hung up the phone and it rang again. It was Phil. They talked for over an hour. Mair was so glad he called because she wanted him to know he should call her cell phone the weekend she would be visiting her aunt. Not only that, she told Phil about her moving tomorrow and hadn't yet made arrangements to have the phone installed in her new home and didn't want to miss his calls.

During the previous week, each day Mair brought some of her belongings to the new house. This day is the day she will move into her own home. Very early in the morning she loaded the car for the final move. Mair had taken the morning off from work to get settled in her new home. The Murphy's had a two-car garage, however one was packed full of "God knows what" is Mister Murphy's description. Nonetheless Mair was able to use the driveway and parked in front of "God knows what garage door" She finished unloading the car put things in their new place before she washed up and walked to work.

On her way home that evening, she stopped at the local grocery store and bought as much as she could carry home. When she got to her front door, there stood a huge bouquet of flowers. She unlocked her door balancing her grocery bags but didn't have the extra hand to carry in the flowers. The Murphy's, sitting on their front porch, heard her struggling so, Mr. Murphy went downstairs, carried in her flowers and said, "Somebody sure loves you," as he set the bouquet on her counter.

She put the groceries away, while nibbling on some of the fruit she just bought. Then she opened her bouquet which contained two dozen American beauty roses. The card read, "To the most beautiful American beauty of them all-with all my love-Phil." She sat down looking at the roses and wishing he was sitting next to her right now. A surprisingly lonely feeling filled her whole body. What surprised her more than anything was she never felt this kind of lonely before. She wanted to speak to Phil and it was difficult not to. However she knew Phil would've called her if he had the opportunity. It was late before Mair got into bed, but she was restless and couldn't fall asleep. She got up, made herself a cup of tea, turned on the TV and sat on the couch.

The week went by fast with working and shopping for all the odds and ends needed. Her mom and dad stopped by and Mair insisted they stay for dinner. The next day Lyn and a couple of her friends were parked in front of the house, waiting for Mair to come home. The friends were Lyn's soccer teammates so they had a lot to talk about wanting to follow MaryRose's reputation. It was midweek when Phil called and Mair never did make dinner because they talked on the newly installed phone for a couple hours. She was glad he called for a number of reasons. One being she wanted Phil to know this was the weekend she would be at the convent to see her Aunt. Mair told him all the little things she had bought for the house and couldn't wait until he was back in DC to see what she did. "Is that the only reason why you want me to come back to DC?" Phil asked.

"Well," Mair hesitated before saying, "there might be one or two other reasons. I can't wait to see you and before I forget though, thank you so much for the flowers. They are beautiful and if you get home in time they might still be in bloom. Do you have any idea when that will be?"

"As things stand now, hopefully I'll be home the weekend after you see your Auntie Marge. I'll keep you posted though. I can't wait; I need to hold you close to tell you how much I miss you."

Mair was able to get off work on Friday an hour earlier to leave for the Sisters of the of the Angels convent. It will be different this time. The novitiates that were there when Mair was are almost ready to take their final vows to become nuns. She wondered if all of women did take the final vows. There were one or two who were struggling before she left. Mair was excited though to see her Auntie Marge, who always has meant so much to her.

Mair arrived at the convent's garden gate just before dark and Sister Joel unlocked the gate for her.

"I'm sorry, Sister Joel. I forgot the gates are locked at night, or I would've made a point to get here earlier."

"Oh, it's perfectly all right Sister MaryRose. Come with me; your Aunt is very anxious to see you." Auntie Marge was standing at her office door, waiting to give her niece a big hug. She asked Sister Joel if she would bring a cup of tea for both Sister MaryRose and her.

"No, Auntie Marge she doesn't have to get the tea, I can go to the kitchen and get it myself." Sister Joel would hear none of it. She was on her way to the kitchen and a few minutes later the tea was brought to the Mother Superior's office. While the two women sipped their tea, Auntie Marge was anxious to get caught up on her niece's comings and goings and they talked over an hour. At one point, Mair asked her Aunt, "I've noticed you and Sister Joel both referred to me as Sister MaryRose, I don't understand why."

"Actually my dear, shall I say - on the books, you are still considered a novice."

"How come? I didn't get to take my first vows,"

"No, you didn't. As we both know when you heard Mattie died you left. The office at the convent never was informed one way or the other whether you were coming back. Until there is some official notification of your intent you are Sister MaryRose."

"I had no idea, or I would've talk to you long before this. As you know, Mattie's death affected me more than I can explain. You knew she meant the world to me, actually she was my world most of my life.

Mair continued talking, "Auntie Marge I never knew anybody who died, certainly no one who was so close to me. I was completely distraught and had no idea how to handle grief. It took me a long time to open up and face the reality of death. Even now as I talk about Mattie there's a lump in my throat."

"Believe me, Mair I understand. Everyone handles grief in a different way and as far as I know there is no right or wrong way to grieve. So don't punish yourself. However you did not handle the situation of your leaving days before you were to take vows by not talking to me first and letting me know what your plans were. I realize at the time you left you had no idea what your plans were, but you should have notified the convent once you did have plans."

"Yes, and I felt ashamed. I really wasn't sure how to face you. I am truly sorry and hopefully I have grown and learned how to act. Tell me, are all the girls I started out with as novices about to take their final vows?"

"There will be six taking their final vows in a few weeks. One girl left shortly after she took her first vows and the other gal left about six months ago."

"I would love to see those who are left. Will I be able to tomorrow?"

"Of course we'll arrange to have lunch together tomorrow." Auntie Marge agreed and then said. "Do you have intentions to remain Sister MaryRose at this point?"

"I have learned so much from you in the past, particularly when I was having so much difficulty making decisions and I think I am much better these days, but I don't want to make this decision right now, as long as I don't have to and it is with your permission.

MaryRose sat in front of the Mother Superior wanting to give her a definitive answer, but felt she needed more time and also needed to pray a great deal. Finally, she said, "I do have intentions of coming back but at this time I have mixed emotions I feel if I ask God for the answer He will show me the way."

"Very well, for the time being we will leave it at that. I will ask you to keep me informed and certainly, if you're intentions change." MaryRose got up from her chair and knelt before her Aunt and held both of her hands promising not to let her down.

MaryRose had a very fitful sleep. She had a feeling her aunt was well aware of Phil being in her life. Her Mother and aunt spoke on the phone regularly and Mair couldn't imagine her Mother not mentioning MaryRose seeing this young man. Plus the fact, Mair knew her father would love to see his daughter and Phil marry. It's strange she thought how words aren't always needed to know what other people feel.

In the morning she showered and dressed before going to early morning mass in the Chapel. Mair felt comfortable and at peace as she heard Mass. She recalled the many times they prayed together in the Chapel. By ten in the morning, all the novices and nuns in the convent went into the dining room where there was a huge round table that seated all the nuns and novices headed by a chair for the Mother Superior. This morning, an extra chair had been placed next to the Mother Superior for Sister MaryRose. The six novices ready to take their first vows were glad to see MaryRose again, as MaryRose was to see them. Sister Joel and several of the other nuns prepared a delicious breakfast.

Later that afternoon, MaryRose and Auntie Marge sat out in the arbor as they had done many times before. They chatted a bit before MaryRose said she would have to be on her way. She had told her Aunt where she was working and living, and how close it was to Georgetown and her Mother's work. Sister Joel came outside with a box of goodies for MaryRose to take home. "Oh, thank you so much. I haven't had time to do any baking yet so these will be wonderful to have in the house and are very much appreciated."

As MaryRose drove home, she knew she had much to think about. She prayed for help and making the right decisions. The late Sunday afternoon in DC traffic was minimal, so the trip home was shorter than usual and pleasant. Once settled in her apartment, she noticed several messages on the cell phone. She had left the cell phone in the glove compartment of the car in order not to be disturbed at the convent. One was from her Mom, another from Fred her officemate and the last was from Phil. Her Mother wanted her to call when she got home and Fred asked Mair to come into the office a little earlier than usual because he had an appointment. Phil left a phone number and she called it soon as she arrived home. She called her mom and then Fred to assure him she'd be in the office early.

Mair punched the numbers in her cell phone which Phil had given her. Her heart started to pound in her chest anticipating hearing Phil's voice. Phil did not answer, rather another special agent - special agent, Thompson. Mair asked to speak to Phil Kern and seconds later, "You're home MaryRose," Phil asked, and before she could answer, "Stay right there. I'll call you back within ten minutes, don't go away."

Mair got up and poured herself a glass of iced tea, went back to the living room, sat on the couch and watched the minutes pass until the phone rang, "Phil, I hope this is you."

"Oh, it's good to hear your voice Mair. I can't talk long I'm in a business meeting, out of the hearing range of the agents. I just found out today I'll be home this Thursday, and I cannot wait to see you. You know what, Mair, more than anything else in this world my only hope is you feel the same."

145

"I should keep you guessing, but I can't. I do want to see you as soon as possible."

"I miss you Mair more than I've ever missed anybody in my life. Stay with me forever."

"Come home to me and you'll know how much I've missed you." With that, the phone went dead. Mair just stared at the phone and in her heart she knew she was falling in love with Phil. Yet just this afternoon, she was expressing her love of God to Auntie Marge. She knows you can't fool God and it would break her heart to fool Phil. Tears welled in her eyes and she began to cry bitter tears. In her sobbing, she begged God to give her some sign- some way she'd know what He wanted her to do.

Mair got to the office earlier than usual as promised. She no sooner got there and phones were ringing and one of her clients arrived. She had to put her own problems aside and try to solve her client's problems.

At lunch time Mair met her Mother and they lunched together in the Georgetown Café

"Mair, it is so good to see you. I have to tell you, you're very much missed," her Mother said as soon as she saw her daughter.

"I miss you guys too, and there are times in my apartment I could scream because it's so quiet, and yet I must admit there are also times I love the solace. By the way, how is Gracie working out?"

"She truly is a charm, the same temperament as Mattie, you know, cool and collected. Your sister really gets along with her too. And I have to tell you, she's a fantastic cook, certainly as good as our Mattie."

"I'm glad to hear that. I'll have to stop by and get some lessons from her."

Marianne asked her about Auntie Marge and their time together. Mair became sullen.

"Mair did I say something wrong?" her Mother question. But Marianne knew her daughter was obviously upset. She could see the tears in her eyes. "MaryRose, something's bothering you and you know there's nothing you can't tell me. Sometimes it's better to talk than hold our problems within."

"Oh, Mom, I am so confused and I don't seem to know what I want or what's the best thing is for me. I just don't know, what is wrong with me?"

"What are you battling with, Mair? Is it a vocation with God or a different kind of vocation with Phil?"

"You see my problem, mother, so why can't I realize that's the core of my problem?"

"Sometimes MaryRose, we are so close to a problem we can't see exactly what the problem is. I can't tell you what to do, all I can advise you is to follow your heart. I honestly believe if you do that you'll find happiness...the happiness you are meant to have. Perhaps you should stop fighting and let the decision make itself." The two women talked a little longer before it was time for both to return to work. MaryRose gave her Mother a hug and a kiss and thanked her for always being there.

The next few days seemed to drag for Mair, because every minute that passed was a minute closer to seeing Phil. Finally Thursday was here and Mair dressed in a strikingly blue sheath which accented the red in her auburn hair. She didn't know when to expect Phil only that he was going to be home today. She went to hear mass at the Georgetown church, which she had been doing every morning since coming home from the convent before going to the office. "Wow, look at you. Miss Gillian, you look fantastic in that color. Maybe we should put you in the window. That would really attract clients," her employer Gerry remarked.

The office was busy but not because of MaryRose's blue dress; however Gerry disagreed. Shortly after three

147

Jane Caracci

p.m. MaryRose looked out the window and Phil was looking in the window. She got up from her desk and Phil opened the door and they embraced. Everyone in the office, including the clients, gave them a standing ovation.

CHAPTER FOURTEEN

Phil and Mair walked hand-in-hand to Mair's apartment. The Murphy's were sitting on their front porch and watched them coming down the street. As they got closer to the house, Mr. Murphy asked, "Hi there, is this the gentleman who loves roses? MaryRose laughed as she nodded her head. She introduced Phil to the Murphy's before they entered her apartment.

"I can't believe the roses are still alive," Phil noted, but quickly had Mair wrapped in his arms. "I'm really having a hard time keeping my hands off of you. While I was away, I dreamed of this moment. Do you have any idea how much I care for you?"

"I think I do, because this is all I thought about while you were gone," MaryRose admitted. They walked through the apartment and Mair showed Phil the new double size bed he hadn't seen before he left for New York. They sat on the end of the bed and Phil kissed her like she had never been kissed before. She started to unbutton his shirt and before long they both lay on the bed naked in each other's arms. They made love like Mair never imagined love could be. She knew at that moment this was the man she truly loved. She looked into his eyes, "I've never told anybody before, but I am in love with you."

"I've waited a long time to hear those words from you."

"For whatever reason and I really don't know why, to tell somebody I loved them has never been easy for me to say, and I never have said them to anyone before, but today it was easy and real to say them to you." Mair started to laugh and asked Phil, "Sometimes I think I need a psychiatrist, do you think so?"

"No, all I ever want is you to need me."

"Do you think your boss Gerry will give you tomorrow off so we can have a nice long weekend before I go back to work Monday?" Phil asked.

"Probably so," Mair said as she picked up the phone and questioned, "Sue is Gerry still in the office?"

"Oh MaryRose he just left, but he told me to tell you in case you called, to please take tomorrow off" MaryRose laughed and thanked her and said to Phil," I didn't know I was so transparent, but we have the whole weekend to be together." They went out for a quick bite to eat and returned to the love bed.

The following morning Phil decided it was high time he had a change of clothes, so the plan of the day was to go out to his house on the outskirts of DC. Mair didn't have any idea of what to expect, mainly because Phil seldom spent any time there. The trip out, took about thirty to forty minutes, Mair wondered if Phil thought about his wife. She knew this must have been a very difficult for him, even though it was some time ago. When they arrived there, all Mair could think of was what a beautiful honeymoon cottage. The thing that impressed her the most was a beautiful garden along the white picket fence. "Phil, this is lovely, who cares for all of this while you are away?"

"An old FBI agent, who is long retired, lives on the next block and offered to do the upkeep of the garden and keep an eye on the house. Larry is a neat old gent and he takes a load off my mind. I keep thinking I should sell the house, but somehow it never gets done. Larry tells me there are any number of people ready to buy." The inside was as lovely as the garden. MaryRose wondered if the memory of his wife was the reason he did not let it go. Phil was busy in the bedroom collecting some of his clothes, but Mair didn't go in feeling it was an intrusion.

"Hey, where are you?" Phil called out but before she could answer, the doorbell rang. Phil came out of the bedroom saying, "I bet that's Larry now. He sees a car in the driveway and he is here checking up. Sure enough, Phil opened the door and it was like two best friends who hadn't seen each other in a long time. "How are you doing Larry; it's good to see you, come on in." As Larry walked in, he saw MaryRose

"Now Phil, I need an introduction to this beautiful lady."

The three chatted a few minutes and Larry indeed made MaryRose feel very comfortable. The two men talked about things that were needed to be done around the house. Phil agreed and gave Larry a blank signed check.

They hadn't been on the road very long when Phil pulled in front of a delicatessen. "I'll only be a few minutes," he said and entered the deli. A few minutes later he came out with a huge bag, and said, "Now my lady, let's go to Rock Creek and have a picnic." It was such a beautiful day and Rock Creek Park with its blooming flowers made it perfect for their picnic.

"You amaze me Phil; you bought everything I love to eat. How did you know?"

"You're too important not to remember all the things you love." Mair leaned across the table and gave him a big kiss on his lips. After their lunch, they walked hand-in-hand through the park before returning to Mair's house. Again during the ride Mair was quiet, unusually quiet. So when they got in the house, the first thing Phil asked, "Mair, tell me what's on your mind."

"Why do you ask?"

"You've been very quiet since going to my house. I know you well enough to know something's bothering you. So let's talk."

"I guess you do know me well, but it wasn't something that was bothering me, Phil. Seeing your lovely home that you and your wife shared a relatively short time made me wonder how was it for you to go to your house with another woman. I guess what I'm trying to say is how do you erase those memories? Do you think about the years gone by? I guess I felt I was intruding"

Phil sat there quietly and listening to MaryRose he realized the woman he loved now was a very deep and caring woman; the kind of woman he always wanted but never had. Finally he said, "My dear MaryRose, the love I had for Kerry was a true love. However, not the love I have for you. The love for Kerry was a young love and it never had a chance to grow into something deep and strong. So the house we went to today was my house, not our house, not Kerry and Phil's house. Certainly not a house where you would be an intruder." He walked over to her and put his hands on her shoulders and looking straight into her eyes he said, "Today Mair you showed me the reason why I love you more than anything in this world." Tears welled in her eyes as the couple embraced. Mair whispered in Phil's ear,

"Thank you Phil for showing me what real love is; now I can be sure I love you."

Together they cooked dinner and the enjoyment they found in each other was unmistakable. Just as the couple finished dinner the phone rang. Mair answered the call, "hi

Mom," and talked for several minutes. "That was my mother when she didn't get any answer last night she wanted to make sure all was well. Then she found out you were back in town Phil, so mom asked us to come out for a cookout Sunday. I told her I'd get back to her. I wanted to know how you felt about it.

"If that's what you want Mair, sounds great to me."

"Good, I'll call Mom in the morning and tell her we're coming."

Phil and MaryRose spent a wonderful weekend together. They went to museums and the theater, took long walks along the Potomac, and even rented kayaks, which they raced against each other. It should be noted MaryRose won the race. All Phil said was "I should've known better." After mass on Sunday, they drove across the bridge to MaryRose's parents' home for brunch. MaryRose had never met Gracie who immediately reminded her of Mattie. She mentioned the fact to her Mom who readily agreed. After seeing Phil for a short time at their first meeting, Bill Gillian was pleased to see him again. For whatever reason, Phil impressed Bill and was anxious to know more about this man who obviously impressed his daughter. On the other hand, MaryRose's mother believed her husband was so impressed hoping this is the man his daughter would marry. They weren't there very long before Chuck and Christine arrived as Lyn was flying down the stairs wondering why no one woke her up earlier.

The entire family was sitting on the sun porch sipping mimosas as Gracie announced brunch was ready in the dining room. When Phil saw the display of food on the buffet he immediately put his arm around Gracie and offered her a job. "Sorry my friend, Gracie is spoken for," Bill Gillian announced. Everyone served themselves and sat around the table, including Gracie who sat next to Phil, pleasing him. He winked at Mair's Father, but pointed his finger to himself. After the delicious buffet, everyone swore they wouldn't be able to eat for a couple of days. Bill and Marianne joined the young ones at the tennis court. The parents sat in the shade to watch "the kids" play tennis. Phil, who hadn't played tennis in years, tried to bribe Lyn to take his place. It didn't work so Chuck and Christine slaughtered Mair and Phil. Bill Gillian warned Phil, "You better get practicing young man if you want to compete here." Phil looked at Mair and apologized for letting their team down and promised to do better, but under his breath he whispered in Mair's ear "Maybe it will happen in my next life."

On the drive back to Mair's house, they both commented on what a great time they had at the Gillian home and how it climaxed a perfect weekend together. "The thought of work tomorrow doesn't make me happy," Mair mentioned.

"I know just what you mean. I have to go out to Quantico to report my assignment and find out what's next."

"Phil, do your assignments always take you out of town?"

"That's a hard question to answer. Some definitely do, some are right here in DC or Quantico, and some are out of the country." Phil answered.

"I guess in your business that makes sense. When I think about it, I've never seen you more than a few days at a time and the times in between could be as long as a year. I've never really thought about it before."

"MaryRose what makes you think about it now?"

"Probably because early on we were not even friends and now we have strong feelings," Mair laughed. "It's amazing how time changes many emotions and suddenly our friendship grew in a direction neither one of us ever thought."

"Well, now you're speaking for yourself."

"I am. I don't understand."

"I know when I was recruiting at Notre Dame, you thought I was a pain in the neck, and for that matter, for several years after. You must have realized I had some kind of interest in you. I must admit, up until you were going to college in England, I had tried to recruit students of your caliber. I thought you would be an outstanding candidate, a candidate you seldom see at the college level. When you came back to Harvard, I realized what I thought was a platonic relationship, was more."

"At that point, were you still interested in my becoming a candidate for the FBI?"

"The best way to answer you. MaryRose is to tell you, if you are interested in becoming an FBI agent it would be great, but if your interest is in practicing law in a law firm, whatever you want as a profession would be fine. What I want for you is your happiness." Mair looked at Phil and smiled. Phil parked the car in front of Mair's apartment and said, "Here we are and I better get my things together."

"Oh, you have to leave tonight?" Mair asked

"I really should Mair; I have to be in Quantico first thing tomorrow morning."

"Okay, let's go in and we'll have a bite to eat. I don't know about you but I just want something light. I'm still full from Gracie's brunch." Phil didn't dispute the point.

While Mair was cleaning up the kitchen, Phil went into bedroom to gather up his belongings. When both finished their chores, Phil put his overnight case by the front door. Mair got up from her chair and walked towards him and he towards her. They embraced, with a long passionate kiss. Mair made it clear she did not want him to leave although she was fully aware he had no choice. Phil told her he wasn't sure when he'd be able to call, but at first chance he would.

The minute Phil walked out the front door, Mair missed him.

She sat in her living room for a long time reliving their weekend together. For a long time after that, she wondered what her future held. She kept thinking, *what do I really want in my life - is it Phil - is it the law - is it the church.* Mair sat up most of the night writing down lists of pros and cons; under Phil, practicing law and taking final vows. When her reasoning was finished she really hadn't come to any specific conclusion. Mair got up and made herself a cup of coffee and looked at the lists again and again trying to figure out what was missing. Under all three lists headings the words "I love" were there. She loved Phil, she loved the law and she loved the church, and yet there was something missing. "What is it, what is missing?" Mair screamed, "What is the missing link?"

Mair got herself another cup coffee and started to think about Phil again. She got to thinking about Phil's life and his work in the FBI. Whereas he never talked about what he actually was doing, but he did talk about all the different places he goes and the people he meets She thought about these things and realized how content Phil was with his life and how he found so much interest in his job. And suddenly the thought came to her, *Is this what I should be doing*? The more she thought about it, she became excited. Mair lay down on the couch with a thousand questions crowding her mind. She thought about the pros and cons of the decision to apply to the FBI. It wasn't long before Mair fell asleep until she was awakened by her phone ringing. It was her office wondering if she was all right and if she was coming into work. Mair, trying to orient yourself to the day and time, finally said, "Sue, I'm so sorry. I- I overslept, what time is it? I'll be in shortly. I'm so glad you called."

"No problem MaryRose, you take your time and we'll see you in a while."

Mair jumped in the shower, threw on some clothes, gulped

down a glass of orange juice, grabbed an apple, and was out the door. She was all apologies when she got to the office, but no one seemed upset. It was a busy Monday morning, which probably was good, giving MaryRose little time to do more thinking of her decision of last night, rather early this morning. Her work day went by quickly and by the time she unlocked her front door she felt she was ready for bed.

She was awakened the next morning by the phone ringing. Her first thought it was Phil, but it was her mom asking, "How about meeting me for lunch later?" They settled on the time and restaurant before their goodbyes.

MaryRose looked around the apartment and started picking up all the papers scattered all over the living room. As she gathered them up she glanced at some of the papers and smiled. *It took all this paperwork to finally make a decision. Oh Phil, please call soon. There's so much I want to talk to you about.*

Before meeting her Mother, Mair decided not to mention anything about the FBI until she talked to Phil. She did thank her for the wonderful time they had at Sunday brunch and how thrilled she was Gracie was part of the family. "MaryRose, I just have to ask, are you serious about Phil? Now I know it's none of my business and you don't have to answer, but I am curious," her Mother smiled.

"I have very strong feelings for Phil and I think he has the same for me. How serious we are, or where it's headed, I can't answer that right now. I'm not putting you off, Mom; I'm just telling you how it is today."

A week passed before Mair received a phone call from Phil telling her he was in Seattle, Washington. "I miss you honey and hopefully I'll see you soon."

"Oh, I hope so Phil, I have so much I want to talk to you about. Will you be in Seattle for long?"

"This is just an in and out job and I should be leaving Thursday. How about we have a date night on Friday?" Mair readily agreed and Phil replied, "Great, I'll call you when I get in. I can't wait to hear all the news you have to tell; you sure sound excited."

"I am Phil, I'm very excited." Mair's excitement peaked by their date night. Phil called Mair just before she left the office. He had just gotten off the plane and wanted her to give him a couple of hours to get cleaned up. He'd pick her up by seven o'clock. Mair got home from work and showered and put on her striking blue dress and literally stood watch for Phil's car at the window. As soon as the car pulled up to the curb, Mair opened the door and when Phil took those three steps down he took one look and wrapped her in his arms.

"You are one beautiful woman to come home to and I'm one lucky man." The two walked arm in arm into the apartment. Phil sat down on the sofa and Mair knelt on the floor in front of him, "If this is a proposal – my answer is yes."

"Phil, when you left last Sunday I spent the entire night trying to figure what, where and when I wanted for my life. So, I made three lists; the first was headed by you, the second was law and the third was the church. Under each heading, I wrote the pros and cons that I valued and what I wasn't interested in. Each column ended with the word love. In other words, I love you, the law, and the church and yet in the end, I realized there was something missing. Somewhere there is a missing link. I tried to sleep, but sleep wouldn't come. I got another cup of coffee and paced the living room floor, trying to find what the missing link is. I started thinking about you again and how I admired the way you conduct your life. You are doing what you love, seeing the world, meeting new people, solving problems to their conclusion. Suddenly, I knew what was missing. I was jealous of your life and finally decided how I could make it my life. Phil, after all these many years your recruiting has come full cycle – I want to become an FBI agent. Show me the way."

Phil was stunned. He sat there for a few moments not able to say anything. There was this beautiful lady kneeling before him to tell him she wanted to be an FBI agent. Did he hear her right? "MaryRose, I thought I knew you well, but you continually amazed me. I would've given anything to hear those words over the years I was recruiting you."

"You're not happy now?"

"Yes - I am. I am for you and then again I'm not sure for me."

"I don't understand Phil. Over the years we have developed a wonderful relationship. I thought you would be delighted. Finally, you won me over." Mair said confused.

"MaryRose, we do have a wonderful relationship and it's no secret that I want to marry you. We've talked about marriage between agents in the FBI and how difficult it is to keep a marriage together, when get together time is often a rarity. On the other hand, my dear Mair, you are a rarity. If this is what you want, I'm with you one hundred percent" She got off of her knees and cuddled in his lap.

"Auntie Marge always told me that God would show me the way. Through you Phil, He has shown me the way. I have finally found love and how to show that love." The couple sat on the couch for several more hours discussing what the future will be for both of them. Their Friday night date night at a special restaurant turned out to be a late-night snack at the local café. They continued making plans on their return to the apartment. Suddenly, Mair started laughing and said, "Actually, Phil, I am still Sister MaryRose."

"Well, to my knowledge there's never been a nun as an FBI agent, but there's always the first time," Phil smiled.

"Rather than talk to Auntie Marge over the telephone, I really need to go to the convent. If possible,

Phil, I'd love you to come with me. I think my aunt will have a better understanding of my decision when she sees you."

"Let me check my schedule on Monday and we'll make a plan. I've heard so much about this remarkable woman, I look forward to meeting her. On the other hand, when you tell your father, I don't think I should be there; he might throw me head first into the pool." The rest of the weekend the two relaxed while spending a great deal of time talking FBI. Phil made it clear he wanted to present her credentials to the board of applicants personally. In the meantime, Mair was to gather all her credentials, accolades, and awards, plus her scholastic review.

The following Friday, Mair and Phil drove to the Sisters of Angels convent. Sister Joel greeted them in the garden and led them to the Mother Superior's office.

She was thrilled to see her niece and to meet Phil Kern. She had heard a lot about Phil from her sister so really wasn't surprised to see him now. Sister Joel brought in a platter of tea sandwiches and cookies along with the pot of tea for all. Auntie Marge talked directly to Phil and asked many questions about his life. They were there about an hour before the subject at hand was finally approached. MaryRose took a deep breath and said, "Auntie Marge I came here today to tell you, I'm going to decline my vocation and taking first vows." You could hear a pin drop in the room. The nun, or anyone for that matter, didn't say a word.

"My dear Sister MaryRose, I accept your decision with all my love."

"Without your love and understanding and wisdom I couldn't have made the decision to apply to the FBI."

"Oh my," her aunt gasped, "that I wasn't expecting." As if she just remembered Auntie Marge turned to Phil and asked, "Are you the young man who bothered my niece with recruiting her at every opportunity you had?"

"Yes I plead guilty, but I must admit it was pleasure because I came to know your remarkable niece."

"Do I sense there might be more to this relationship than the FBI?" Mair's aunt smiled.

"Auntie Marge, I do confess I have fallen in love with Phil and I want you to love him too, because I'm convinced God sent him to me. May I show Phil your chapel?" The three said a prayer in the chapel and went out in the garden before leaving. Auntie Marge gave her niece and Phil her blessings and asked they keep in touch.

As they were driving back to Washington, Mair looked at her watch and said. "It's almost four o'clock, why don't I call my parent's house. Neither of my parents should be home yet, but I'll call Gracie and asked her to put two more place settings on for dinner tonight."

"Sounds good to me, but are you planning to tell your parents about the FBI?"

"Might as well Phil; my Dad certainly isn't going to bite you. Plus I'm so excited I really want them to share our excitement." Phil warned her it might be the end of his life. She laughed and dialed the phone. Gracie answered and Mair told her the plan and asked her not say a word to anyone; she wanted it to be surprise. Phil pulled the car into the Gillian's driveway around six o'clock, and Mair's father pulled in the driveway right behind them. With the exception of Gracie, everyone was surprised and happy to see them.

"What's the occasion?" Mair's Father asked.

"We - well, actually I have something exciting tell you," Mair answered and from the look on her father's face she was sure he thought it was about wedding bells. So to stop the illusion immediately, she said, "Let's all go sit on the sun porch and have a cocktail and I'll tell you right away."

As they toasted each other, Phil got up and stood by the sun porch door while Mair said, "Mom, Dad, Lyn and Gracie, I have decided to apply to the FBI as soon as possible." Dead silence prevailed. Finally her Dad wanted to know if that's why Phil was ready to run away. They all laughed and wanted to hear about her plans. Phil inched his way back into the room and joined Mair explaining her decision. Mair's excitement was obvious to all and her Father said, "What better way to practice international law."

CHAPTER FIFTEEN

When Phil and Mair got back to her apartment, Phil sat down with Mair and explained what she should expect in applying to the FBI. "I know many of the guys at the main office downtown DC who will be doing a lot of interviewing and presentations for new applicants. They are a good bunch of guys, very fair, but they don't slip up on anything. "I'll find out tomorrow the timing of your application. There's a possibility a lot can be bypassed, but there is much that cannot be. Hopefully I'll be able to monitor your progress through the process. When I get back tomorrow morning I'll get my schedule and find out when it will be possible for you to start the application process. I will call you at your office as soon as I have the information."

"Phil, I can't tell you how excited I am. I really appreciate your helping and as you could plainly see Dad and Mom are hundred percent on your side."

They talked late into the night, mostly of what lies ahead for Mair. Finally, Mair suggested they better get some sleep. She went in to take a quick shower and it wasn't long before Phil entered the shower with her. They bathed together, dried off their bodies and then made love, which reached a beautiful climax. They lay in bed with their arms around each other Phil leaning on his elbow, looked into

Mair's beautiful face and said, "I know my dear, after tomorrow, our lives will change."

"You mean they'll change for the better?" Mair questioned.

"I hope so darling. You know we will be often in different directions, even different countries, but together or apart, we must always remember this night and the love we share for each other." These words brought tears to Mair's eyes.

"Promise me Phil, I'll always know where you are no matter how close or far away we'll be from each other." Phil kissed her and they made love again.

Mair anxiously waited to hear from Phil as she sat at her desk in the office. She hadn't told anyone at the office about her joining the FBI, even though she was dying to share the information. She hadn't heard from Phil in the morning so asked Sue to bring her back a sandwich when she came back from lunch. She didn't want to chance missing Phil's call. Actually, it didn't come until mid-afternoon. "Sorry, honey it's taken me so long, but it's been a hectic morning over here. I finally got to speak to Mr. Brad Hampton who will be your coordinator in this phase of the application. You'll get along well with Brad; he's a neat guy. He's going to start your application process as a single so hopefully you can catch up with the next Quantico class."

"When do I start?" Mair breathlessly asked

"Right now it's a go for the 27th of September, which is about 10 days away. Don't say anything to the crew at the office just yet. Brad wants to get a confirmation on the date, which will be either late this afternoon or early in the morning."

"Sounds perfect. Are you able to come over for dinner tonight?"

"As things are working out, I should be working here at the downtown office for three or four days so I'll definitely see you later and we can grab a bite someplace." Mair decided rather than going out to eat, she'd pick up something to cook at home. Before closing time at the office, she called Gracie and asked her for a recipe for a quick dinner. A few minutes later Gracie came up with a steak stir-fry which sounded delicious and better yet, easy to make. Mair picked up what was needed on her way home and immediately started cutting up the ingredients the recipe called for. By the time Phil arrived at the apartment he smelled the great aroma of something cooking.

After their home-cooked meal was eaten, Mair had many questions about her interview with Brad. Phil said he couldn't really tell her too much because he was sure there are many changes in interviews since he applied. One thing he was sure of though, she would need a photo of her driver license and will be fingerprinted first thing. And by all means, do not bring anything with you while doing phase one and two, such as smart phones, no kind of textbook, newspaper, reference material, pencils or pens; in other words, nothing. "Before you take any written tests, no doubt you'll see a film stressing both the significance of special agent as well as potential dangers an agent might face. But let's stop talking FBI; how about we take a walk. It's such a beautiful night.

When they came back to the house, Mr. and Mrs. Murphy were sitting on the front porch and asked them to join them for a glass of wine. The Murphy's were really very pleasant people, and never questioned the relationship between their tenant and Phil. It was obvious they liked both of them. They once mentioned having their own children and grandchildren and the world was a different place since they were young. "They all are grown now and doing their own thing and we keep our fingers crossed they're doing the right thing. At our age," Mr. Murphy said. "We just sit here on our porch and are thankful for them all."

As anxious as Phil was not to talk about the FBI, he wanted to be sure Mair was aware of the grueling testing she was about to face in phase one and two. "Honey, it really can get you down because it's non-stop."

"Tell me Phil when you were going through what I'm about to go through, did you find it over the top and difficult to go through?" She wanted to know.

"As I remember, I did a hell of a lot of sweating, and I wasn't as confident or smart as you. Plus the fact is you've already had a lot of world experiences, where I was a Midwestern country boy.

I know MaryRose; you are going to amaze your testers. I'm willing to bet it's a rare occasion they meet up with a woman like you."

"You don't think Maybe you are a little prejudiced? Mair smiled.

They weren't back in the house, but a few minutes and the phone rang. Mair answered and listened for a moment and a smile came across her face. She hung up without saying anything, "It was a message, and the twenty-seventh is confirmed. I am to be at the Federal Bureau of Investigation building on Pennsylvania Avenue at eight a.m."

Phil's three remaining days in DC passed quickly. He had research work to do, but spent the evenings and nights with Mair. Little did either one know Phil would be gone several months, somewhere in the Middle East. Phil of course knew his destination. However, the where's and why's of a special agent are never open for discussion. Those three evenings and nights were fun and romantic at the same time. Phil even tried his hand at cooking one night. The meal ended in the garbage so eating at a restaurant seemed like the next best thing to do. Their goodbyes were difficult not knowing how long Phil would be gone and Mair's starting her testing without Phil's moral support.

166

Mair knew as soon as Phil left she would have to tell Gerry and the people at Clarkson Law firm she would be leaving and her plans to be an FBI Special Agent. She thoroughly enjoyed her time at the law firm and even more so, the people she worked with. She felt they would always be friends. Giving her notice was going to be difficult. As soon as she entered the office, she went directly to Gerry's office, knocked and entered. Gerry look surprised to see her; it was unusual for her to come to his office. "Good morning MaryRose, what can I do for you?" MaryRose sat down and pulled her chair close to his desk. "Do you have a secret to tell me? Gerry asked.

"I can't keep it a secret anymore, Gerry. I'll be leaving the law firm on the twenty-seventh of this month. I'll be starting the procedure to file application for a FBI special agent. I will miss all of you here at Clarkson Law. I've enjoyed every minute working here."

Gerry looked across the desk at her with a look on his face as if to say, you've got to be kidding. At first not knowing what to say, he finally said. "Well I'll be damned. I knew MaryRose the day would come you'd be moving on, but I never dreamt it would be to the FBI. A bigger law firm yes, but the FBI, that's a surprise."

The two talked for a few more minutes and then Gerry got up from behind his desk and stood next to MaryRose wishing her all the best. The two entered the outer office and Gerry announced to Fred and Sue, "MaryRose is leaving us to become a very famous FBI agent." There was much laughter since they didn't believe a word of what Gerry said. Eventually MaryRose had a hard time convincing them it was true, but they finally believed her.

At precisely eight a.m. on the twenty-seventh of December, MaryRose walked into the outer office of Mr. Brad Hampton. She announced herself. The woman seated behind the desk notified Mr. Hampton and within minutes Brad Hampton appeared, introduced himself to MaryRose, and said, "My friend Phil was right on the mark in his description of you, Miss Gillian."

"Not knowing his description, Mr. Hampton I'm not sure I should say thank you or just say oh, really."

"Let's just say you should thank him from the bottom of your heart. And now Miss Gillian, please come into my office." As they entered his office, he continued saying he acknowledged her photo driver's license and her fingerprints, as he picked up copies of each sitting on his desk.

"As Phil probably told you I will be your coordinator in the testing of phase one of your application, so therefore call me Brad and I'll call you MaryRose." There was no doubt about Brad putting her at ease immediately. "We'll start off by showing you a film which I understand Phil told you something about."

"It does give you a little insight of what will eventually be expected of you. Understand at any time you can remove yourself from the selection process, if you feel you cannot carry out the duties of an FBI special agent."

MaryRose watched the film with interest and enthusiasm. At its conclusion, Brad told her she would take a three-part test. Number one will be on bio data, number two is inventory testing and the third will consist of forty-seven questions. "Your answers will help us to measure your ability to organize, plan and prioritize, plus how you make judgment decisions, situational judgment, and cognitive ability."

He escorted her into the testing room, where a young man sat at a desk in front of the room, and another was seated in the rear. She answered each question with definitive and precise statements. The testing took many hours and when she was finished, she had to sign a nondisclosure statement and she would hear whether she passed or failed within thirty days. She was escorted to Brad Hampton's outer office and again, Brad was notified of her presence. He came out of his office, looking at his watch, and said, "You took a little above average time to complete the testing."

"I'm going to take that as a good sign because right now my mind is tired of thinking." But then she asked if it would take thirty days or perhaps less to find out her status.

"Because you are the only one present when taking the tests, I would think you will hear probably within a few days or even less. Go home and get a good night sleep."

It wasn't until she heard him say the word sleep she realized how tired she was but also very hungry. She drove to the little Café in Georgetown where she and her Mom and also Phil ate often. It was almost nine o'clock and most of the regular eaters had left. MaryRose didn't mind though; she was too tired to carry on any intelligent conversation. She had a delicious dinner, ordered a cup of soup to take out, and left. In a matter of minutes, she pulled into her driveway. It was dark and she thought she must remember to leave some outside lights on. MaryRose took a quick shower and went to bed, and practically before she hit the pillow, she was sound asleep and didn't wake up until nine o'clock the next morning. She couldn't believe it was so late and jumped out of bed. It took a minute or two before she realized it was okay, she had no place to go anyway.

She decided to occupy her free time doing some good housecleaning. Breakfast over; Mair started her cleaning big time. Since she was a little girl, Mair learned - you take out - you put back, from her Dad. That lesson has followed her over the years, so her cleaning compromised of polishing, dusting, vacuuming and washing the floors. Two hours later, her apartment sparkled. Just as she was thinking of stopping by her Dad's office downtown, the phone rang. "MaryRose this is Brad Hampton, I'm calling to ask you to come to my office before one this afternoon."

"Yes, of course," Mair replied, and then quickly asked, "Is there a problem?"

"Not at all." And the phone went dead. Mair placed the receiver in the cradle and sat there trying to figure out what the conversation was all about. Whatever, it sure was short and sweet. She checked the time; it was eleven o'clock, which gave her time to get cleaned up, dress and have a bite to eat, before driving into the heart of DC.

Mair entered Brad's outer office exactly at a quarter of one. His Secretary announced her arrival and immediately after, Brad came out of his office. He motioned to MaryRose to follow him into a small room composed of a writing table and two chairs. "MaryRose your passing grade from phase one was phenomenal."

MaryRose looked at the man and said, "Are you telling me I passed?"

"I probably shouldn't disclose this; however I think your passing grade will go down in the books as the highest ever achieved. Next on our agenda is this fifteen page application for employment which must be completed within ten days." A broad smile came over Brad's face, "I'm smiling because I'm sure you'll have it done in ten hours; however, you can take as long as ten days." He handed her a packet compiled of fifteen pages. At this point, she was glad Phil had clued her in on this application being judged on the competitiveness of applicants. "You may start here and take as many days as necessary; however, the application cannot be removed from this room." Brad left the room, but reentered a few minutes later. "MaryRose this has nothing to do with your application, but I thought you'd like to know -

well actually, Phil insisted I let you know; Phil is fine and is proud of you and hopes to see you soon."

"Thanks, Brad, I appreciate you telling me." Brad left and Mair opened the package of papers. She immediately read through each page carefully and it was almost four o'clock before she started filling out page by page. She hadn't finished when at five o'clock there was a knock on the door; Brad's assistant, Clara entered.

"Miss Gillian we're about to close this part of the building so just leave your paperwork there. I will lock the door and you will open it, whenever you come back." MaryRose gathered the papers together and the two women walked out of the room. "Do you think you'll be back tomorrow morning?"

"Yes - yes I will. When is the earliest I can come?"

"I'm here at eight a.m. Call and let me know about what time you'll be arriving so I can let the guards know the approximate time of your arrival." Clara said as she was locking her desk. The two women walked together and chatted as they walked out of the building to their respective cars.

The key to this test was to be completely truthful. If you don't pass this test – you're out. It had been a long day, and once MaryRose got home, she had a quick bite, showered and went to bed. The next she knew the six a.m. alarm woke her. After dressing, Mair ate a good breakfast and drove back to DC's down town and immediately went to Brad Hampton's office. Brad escorted her down the hallway explaining she was going to have a polygraph. "This polygraph does not detect lies, but measures the psychological response to different types of questions. The test records continuously and simultaneously changes in cardiovascular, respiratory, and electro dermal which will allow the examiner to give diagnostic opinion of your honesty or dishonesty."

As soon as she entered the room, the tester told her, "I'm going to ask you a set of questions in different order three different times." Providing you have passed all previous testing along with passing the polygraph, you will then be put on the physical readiness list.

Her polygraph testing lasted several hours and was extremely stressful. Mair could not wait to get home to go to bed. It surprised her because all the other testing, although stressful did not take as much out of her. She had been told when the test was over to return to Mr. Hampton's office, which of course she did. Clara told Mair Mr. Hampton would be with her shortly and to please be seated. Shortly turned out to be almost an hour and MaryRose was having a difficult time keeping awake. She got up from her chair and asked Clara, "Is it all right if I walk around the office I'm very stiff from sitting?" Before Clara could answer, Brad came out of his office and motioned for MaryRose to come in.

"MaryRose I have to tell you the testing you have completed the last couple weeks I know has been strenuous and stressful. In spite of that, you have passed each process with unbelievable scores. And you are now on the list of physical readiness. You were given physical requirements early on, which as you know, you passed. In the next few days, there will be an extreme background investigation, which I'm not very concerned about. Compiling all your scores, background investigation, etc. will probably take a week to ten days. When completed you'll be on your way to Quantico, Virginia, where you will endure training challenges unimagined. Even though it will be weeks before you become an FBI special agent it will be well worth the pain."

Brad paused for a minute and then continued.

"It's really been a pleasure to meet you MaryRose and everything Phil told me about you is true. I have to tell you, I had my doubts, but you erased them all."

Brad got up from his chair to shake MaryRose's hand telling her he looks forward to seeing her soon.

"Before you leave, MaryRose I received a communiqué from Phil an hour ago, but it is not for me. It is for you." He handed the folded paper to a smiling lady then said their goodbyes.

As soon as MaryRose got into her car, she read Phil's message. He wrote as this was an FBI delivery he couldn't write his true feelings; however he wanted Mair to know he was following her progress and it was even better than he had predicted. I'm a very proud man, he wrote. He also reminded her to keep up with her workouts and all the things he wanted to say would be possible soon. Signed: Phil Kern

MaryRose sat in the car for a few minutes re-reading Phil's message. She wondered if Phil's "possible soon" was a clue that he would be home soon. MaryRose had no idea she could miss him as much as she does. She began to wonder if she really was ready for Quantico. Brad mentioned this unimaginable training she was about to go through and Phil's reminder to workout made her wonder if she was prepared. As soon as she got home, she called Brad's office and gave Clara her parent's phone number, telling her she would be there for the next few days. She looked at her watch and called home, feeling her Mom would be home by now. Gracie answered the phone and Mair asked to speak to her mother. "Hold on just a minute. Mair, I believe she just pulled into the drive."

"Hi honey," her Mom said breathlessly. "So good to hear from you, Dad and I have been hoping we would see you soon."

"That's exactly why I'm calling you Mom. I finished with all my testing and I have about ten days to wait to get the results of their investigations so I was wondering if I could stay with you guys for a few days. I've been informed the training at Quantico is extremely rigorous so I think I better make sure I'm in really good shape and I can do that easier at your house."

"We would be thrilled to have you here with us. I can't wait to tell Dad, he'll be so pleased. Come right on over."

"It's best I wait until tomorrow morning. I want to speak to Mr. Murphy and explain why I won't be here for a couple of months and pay him the rent. Tell Gracie I should get there around noontime tomorrow. It will be good to be with you and Dad. I can't wait."

It was the dinner hour when she got to her house so MaryRose thought it best to wait a while before seeing the Murphy's. Plus she wanted to clean out her refrigerator and give any perishables she had left to them. About seven in the evening, Mair went upstairs and found the Murphys sitting on their front porch. As always, they were delighted to see her. "You've been a busy lady," Mr. Murphy said. "We only see you when you're coming and going."

"How is that young man of yours; we haven't seen him either?" Mrs. Murphy asked.

"Oh, Alice, you're going to give MaryRose the idea we keep tabs on her comings and goings."

"That's quite all right, Mr. Murphy. It's good to know someone is watching out for me. But I have some news to share with you. I don't know if you knew Phil is a special agent for the FBI and right now is working overseas and hopefully will be home soon. However, I have decided to become an FBI agent myself and of late, I've been at FBI headquarters making application and undergoing intensive phases to get to this point." Both Mr. and Mrs. Murphy were on the edge of their chairs with a look of amazement. "In a little over a week, I will be going down to Quantico, Virginia, where I will have my physical training. Tomorrow I'm going over to my parent's house and will stay there for probably about a week."

The Murphys wanted to know all about her applying and all the training she must do. Mair gladly answered their questions.

She went into her pocket, took out two checks, and handed to them to Mr. Murphy. "I want to pay my rent for the next three months, and ask you to keep an eye on the apartment. If there is anything special you want me to do before I leave, please let me know." The Murphy's assured her they would keep an eye on the apartment and she didn't have a thing to worry about.

After everything was in order at the apartment, the next morning, Mair gathered up the things she would need while staying with her parents and arrived there just before noon. Gracie had already prepared lunch for her, which as always was delicious. "Your Mom told me, you're going to be doing a lot of exercising in preparation for Quantico, so I want you to make a list of the foods you should be eating."

"Good idea. I'll do it right now and then I'll bring my belongings upstairs and go for a run before the family gets home. Thanks so much Gracie. You are an angel sent from heaven."

MaryRose was faithful to her workout routine from six in the morning until five p.m. After taking a shower, she looked forward to having dinner with her family. Some nights it consisted of her Mom and Dad, Gracie, Lyn, and other nights Chuck and Christine joined. No matter who was there, they sat at the dinner table long after the meal was over and enjoyed each other, chatting for hours. On MaryRose's last night the whole family was together. "I have to tell you this past week was wonderful and I thank you all for being part of it and making it a great time. As soon as I hear when I have to leave for Quantico, I'll be sure to let you know. For some reason, I think it's going to be very soon and I'm excited."

"You know my dear we're all rooting for you. You're in our thoughts and prayers and I know you're going to beat the heck out of those guys," her Dad commented. Early the next morning MaryRose pulled into her driveway and another car drove it right behind. She didn't realize a car was behind her at first, but once parked, she looked in the rear view mirror and gasped. She blinked her eyes and jumped out of the car, as Phil got out of his.

They embraced and kissed, "Phil, I can't believe my eyes. When did you get in? That's not important, though. What's important is you're here."

"I've been dreaming of this moment ever since the day I left," Phil whispered.

"I've had the same dream. Let's go in the house."

"MaryRose I only have a few minutes. There's a conference downtown in about twenty minutes." Phil said as he looked at his watch.

"You can come back after the conference?"

"Brad is covering for me right now, so I'm going to run. I'll call you as soon as the conference is over, and mind you, it might be some time. How long I'll be around is questionable, but I should know later on when I call." Phil wrapped her in his arms and kissed her hard and long. Before MaryRose knew what was happening he was gone. She stood there wondering if this was all a dream. She unlocked the back door and entered her dark house. She sat at her kitchen table and re-lived the last few minutes over and over. Several hours later, the phone rang. MaryRose answered on the second ring and heard his voice. Unfortunately, in our excitement we hear what we want to hear. It wasn't long before MaryRose realized it wasn't Phil's voice, rather it was Brad's.

"I'm sorry to disappoint you MaryRose but Phil left on a nine o'clock plane and asked me to call."

"Where is he going?" As soon as she asked, she knew she would not get an answer. "I know

Brad, you can't tell me."

"You're right, but I do have some news to tell you; you leave for Quantico in two days. Come by my office in the morning and I'll give you the transportation tickets and tell you everything you have to know."

"What time do you want me there?" MaryRose asked. Her disappointment came through in her voice. Brad gave her the instructions and suddenly, MaryRose was exhausted.

She arrived at FBI headquarters precisely at seven-fifty the next morning and walked into Brad's outer office at eight. Clara greeted her telling her to go right into Brad's office. He gave her all the instruction she would need for Quantico along with a bundle of fatigues. "I guessed at your size; if I'm wrong they'll make the adjustment at the base." As Brad handed the bundle to her, he took out an envelope and incorporated it in the bundle. "MaryRose, do you have any questions?" MaryRose shook her head. "Remember I'm here and I know you're going to do extremely well. I'll see you back in Washington. He put his hands on her shoulders pulled her closer, as he whispered, "Don't lose anything in that bundle of clothes. Good luck." MaryRose clung tightly to the bundle of clothes; she knew whatever he slipped in between the garments no one else was to see.

"Clara, is it all right if I use your ladies room." Clara nodded and MaryRose entered the bathroom down the hall. She fumbled through the clothes until finally an envelope dropped to the floor. She quickly picked it up, went into a stall, and opened it up sitting on the toilet. She noted immediately it was signed Phil. The note read I'm sorry our moments together were so brief. Just seeing you for those few moments in the driveway, I yearn to be with you. My hope is to see you in Quantico. Always remember, I love you. At the very bottom of the page, Phil wrote, darling, destroy this immediately.

As soon as MaryRose got back to her house, she brought in everything Brad had given her. There were several sets of tops and bottoms and complete rain wear. MaryRose opened her dresser drawer and took out some panties and bras and decided nightgowns were not appropriate for Quantico. She guessed she would be sleeping in her underwear. No cosmetics or hairstyling products would be necessary either. Before she left Brad's office, he explained she would be entering her class at the FBI Academy a week late and this was the reason he gave her clothes and instructions.

She took Phil's crumpled note from her pocket re-read it twice more before burning it. Within seconds, all that was left was ashes. She sat there daydreaming and wondering if the day would come when she and Phil would be partners, FBI partners. When she brought herself back to reality, she read the instructions Brad had given her. Just reading it excited her. She truly was looking forward to her new adventure.

MaryRose thought she would go over to her parents to say goodbye, but on second thought, she decided to give them a call. She had her early morning wake-up to board the train to the FBI Academy in Quantico. She knew it would be four to five months at Quantico. After that was questionable. Her goodbyes were short and sweet to her family. They all were happy for her sensing Mair's excitement.

Once her suitcase was packed and everything was in order in the apartment, she decided to go to her favorite café and get a bite to eat. The phone rang and it was Mrs. Murphy wanting to know if she would come up and have a bite to eat with them. She did and had a memorable evening.

CHAPTER SIXTEEN

MaryRose arrived at Quantico early the next morning. She was directed to the FBI Academy and sent to its head, special agent Sam Wright. After introductions, MaryRose presented her papers to Mr. Wright and was asked to be seated. As he read her report, several times he looked up at her, and then continued reading. "Everything seems to be in order Miss Gillian, and I welcome you here at the FBI Academy. After reading your reports, I'm sure you will do very well. If you have any questions or concerns during your stay here, please let me know."

"Thank you, Sir."

"All candidates are required to complete the basic training here at the FBI Academy, regardless of previous experiences, education, or previous training. You will be considered full time FBI employees. This is the final hiring process. You will be evaluated on every aspect of your training performances including test scores, character, and attitude, before you will be permitted to graduate. I wish you good luck. Mr. Franklin is waiting for you in the lobby and will direct you to your living quarters and then to your training session already in progress.

Living quarters were very much like a large dormitory. Mr. Franklin told her to put on her fatigues and he would meet her at the door facing north. She quickly undressed, put on her fatigues, and hung her clothes in her locker. When she acclimated herself to where north was she met Mr. Franklin, who directed her to the training field. This was the beginning of her excruciating workouts. With a well-trained body she managed to get through them quite well. In her physical training unit, physical fitness was key, along with defense tactics.

MaryRose's team was not only pushed to the limits in physical training, but their training also included practical application, becoming familiar with all firearms the FBI uses, plus investigating methods, intelligence, national security, interrogation methods, and case management, learn white-collar crime, as well as organized crime, trafficking, and domestic and international terrorism, as well as form and development.

By the time twenty-one weeks were almost over, all candidates are familiar and learned of the above, along with behavioral science, social science, and criminal and forensic psychology, crime analysis and problem solving strategies. In conclusion, each candidate will be made aware of all the different avenues special agents can apply themselves. All of the above, including physical training, is renewed during each agent's career.

Male and female candidates are treated equally in all training venues. The only separation was females had their own dormitory. Of the forty-eight women candidates who were in MaryRose's dorm, by graduation thirty-three remained in the program. Of all of them, MaryRose stood out because of her abilities and knowledge. Having said that, she was popular with the women as she always was willing to help and give a hand to any woman in need. Working side-by-side with both men and women day and night, MaryRose felt she had lifetime friends scattered all over the world.

181

Mair kept in touch with her family over the course of her training. Now she could officially tell them she is a FBI special agent with the invitation to her graduation, which was only a few days away on Friday afternoon. She sent Phil's invitation to Brad in Washington DC, saying, if Phil was near enough to please give or send him the envelope.

Graduation was at nine a.m. and there was much hustle and bustle in the dormitories getting ready for the big day. Everyone was to dress in navy slacks, white shirts, and navy ties and black shoes. The graduates assembled on the field at eight-fifteen in the morning and already guests were gathering in the stands. Precisely at nine a.m., the national anthem was played by the Marine Corps band. The huge crowd was in attendance and everyone was straining in the hope of seeing someone they knew. The president of the FBI Academy, retired Colonel Robert Watkins, took the podium. He gave a poignant talk on the value of the FBI in our country. "They are not merely law enforcers; they are protectors of the law and our citizens," the Colonel noted. "They are the watchers of our liberties and keep safe our country. Now these agents have concluded weeks of training, both physical and mental, both of which have been pushed to their limits. I am proud to stand here to give them their badges and credentials, and it is my pleasure as well as honor to swear them in. If all candidates will stand I will do so now." There was a roar of applause as each candidate, now FBI special agents, was given their badge with credentials.

"At this time I want to present the fidelity, bravery and integrity award to a graduating member who the class has selected to receive this award. This year the award unanimously voted by every member of this class goes to Miss MaryRose Gillian." The entire class body stood and clapped, as well as the attending audience. "Miss Gillian, will you please come forward" MaryRose made her way out of the crowded aisle of candidates as Colonel Watkins said, "escorting special agent Miss Gillian is special agent Philip Kern."

Phil waited at the end of the Isle to escort Miss Gillian to the Colonel. Mair took Phil's arm and held it tightly. He escorted her and when they reached the Colonel, Phil stepped back. The uproarious applause was deafening.

"I most humbly accept this award from my classmates. Each and every one has made this experience the most exciting time of my life and I sincerely thank them all for their respect."

MaryRose had a difficult time after walking offstage on Phil's arm. She wanted to hug and kiss him. Plus, she had so much to tell him and so many questions to ask, although that would have to wait because friends and parents were piling out of the stands. Newly awarded special agents gathered around MaryRose to congratulate her. To tell the truth, most were women agents eager to meet MaryRose's handsome escort. Phil spotted Mr. Gillian in the crowd and guided Mair in his direction. Finally, the entire Gillian family was reunited. "How in the world did you all get tickets, I only sent four?" MaryRose asked in amazement.

"Well, your Father felt and rightly so, the entire family should celebrate your accomplishment," her Mother answered.

"Now how in the world having Mom, Gracie plus myself taking up three of the tickets, how do you pick someone out of this crowd to use the fourth - so I got in touch with FBI headquarters in Washington, gave the operator my name and before I knew it I was connected to the office of a Brad Hampton. I introduced myself and told him of my plight." Just as Bill Gillian finished his explanation a young man came over to him and introduced himself,

"Sir, I am Brad Hampton." MaryRose was delighted to see him and gave him a hug, along with a huge thank you.

As the crowd started to thin, and the congratulations thinned out, Mair's Father said, "how about we all go out and get something to eat and take this very special agent home?"

"Dad, there's a reception and buffet in the dining room, plus the fact I cannot leave until tomorrow. It seems Dad, around here they give the orders, and we take orders and comply," as Mair, Phil, and Brad guided the Gillian crowd to the dining room. Mair looked at Phil and whispered, "This has to be one of the happiest days of my life, having you, my family and friends helping me realize a dream come true."

Saturday morning, all the new FBI agents, gathered their belongings and boarded a bus to take them to Mainside Quantico where Phil was waiting to drive his love back to DC. He drove off the base and went down the side road, parked the car and gave Mair a long awaited kiss. Knowing the area well, he drove to a restaurant where their dining lasted over three hours. There was so much to discuss considering Phil has been away for over five months and MaryRose's journey through the FBI Academy. "Where did you apply to do your internship?" Phil asked.

"Headquarters – in DC" Mair answered.

"And you got it?

"Yes and I'm sure we have Brad to thank for my getting it"

"Brad carries a lot of influence, there's no doubt, but getting you a place anywhere is difficult. Especially an internship – There are hundreds of field offices clamoring for new graduates to work for them. He's an amazing guy though and I for one am delighted because once you get out in the field, especially in your international intelligence and interrogation field it can be months before we see each other. We'll be crossing the ocean in different directions."

"I know and I thought a lot about that – I would hate it if we are pulled apart."

"Sweetheart, we've talked about the separations we will have to endure, but we both know if our love is strong we will adjust. Marriage would put the lock on the door, yes, but if we want each other hopefully it's enough."

"Do you really think it will work for us Phil?"

"MaryRose, I just can't answer that. The next two years will be our easiest. You are going to be right here at headquarters and I have asked Brad to try and keep me, at least in the US. Of course, the chances of my being in the DC area all the time is next to nil, but hopefully our times away won't be all that long. What are your feelings?"

"I guess I believe whatever you really want you will get. Neither of us knows what the future brings, so let's embrace the times we are together."

"I agree and right now I have the strongest desire to make passionate love to you." The two opened the front seat doors, closed them, opened the back seat doors, got in, and closed the doors.

Sometime later, they reached Mair's apartment in DC and next to her front door was a huge bouquet of flowers with the card congratulating MaryRose from the Murphy's. After mass the next day, Phil and Mair had one of Gracie's marvelous brunches at the Gillian's. Other than that, they spent their week off just being together coming and going doing whatever struck their fancy. Just being together was all they needed, but like all vacations time passes too quickly and before they knew it, it was the following Monday morning.

They each drove their own cars to headquarters, as Phil was yet to get his next assignment and not knowing where it would be, it was best they both had transportation. Clara was so glad to see MaryRose; she jumped out of her chair and gave her a hug. "I'm so glad you're going to be here for two years, we need somebody like you."

Seconds later, Phil came out of Brad's office and told Mair, "I have good news, I'm going to the field office in Norfolk," as he got closer to her he whispered, "I'll be home every night." Thus, the life of the two FBI special agents began.

During MaryRose's internship at headquarters, most of her work was in law investigations. She found it very interesting as it was something she loved doing and was extremely good at. Phil was checking on field offices all over the states. For the most part, the longest he was away from home was a week; however, more than likely it was no more than overnight. This certainly made their life like any normal couple. Phil did decide to sell his house near the Maryland border. Both he and Mair felt having a place in the DC area, at least for the time being, was more practical. One weekend they went to Maryland and had a garage sale, which turned out to be a weekend party. Larry and other neighbors turned it into a block party.

In Mair's second year at headquarters, she had to decide places she would like to be doing her work. Her forte was certainly international law, but she felt she needed advice. She went up to Brad's offices and asked Clara if she could fit her in for a conference with Brad in the near future. By the next week, Clara called Mair's office downstairs and told her she had an appointment scheduled with Brad for the next day at ten-forty-five in the morning. Mair and Phil had talked about this at some length also, but she felt she needed the objective view Brad would give her.

Brad did just that. He was open, frank, and honest. "MaryRose you have worked long and hard to get to the position you have now. It's time now to accomplish all you worked for. I know your concern is Phil as his concern is for you, but he too must do what he has worked for all these years. I really feel you have something very special so do the things that fulfill your dreams. Remember Phil is doing the same. Someday the two of you will look back and smile and be proud of all you've accomplished."

"I know you are right but sometimes it's difficult to think there might be the possibility of losing what you have now."

"Come on MaryRose, you know changes are prevalent every day of our lives," Brad noted. MaryRose knew he was right and was annoyed with her thinking; she had put indecision as a thing of the past. She browsed thru the papers on possible hot spots and told Brad she would like to do some investigating work in China and her second choice was Israel.

Near the end of her internship and Phil's stateside work at different times, they both reported to Brad's office. First Phil was called in, his next assignment was Turkey, leaving on the third of January, and MaryRose would be going to China, leaving on the fifth of January.

The couple spent the Christmas holidays with Mair's parents and family. It was a joyous time with a note of sadness touched by both Mair and Phil leaving. However, everyone tried to keep the occasion on the light side. There were many laughs. Mair and Phil arrived with arms full of presents many for the latest edition to the Gillian family – Chuck and Christine's baby Sarah who was definitely the center of attention. By this time, Phil had become a family member to all of the Gillian's and Phil felt they were his family, probably due to a lack of his own, but mostly because he was genuinely fond of them all, particularly their daughter. For Christmas, Phil gave MaryRose, a beautiful birthstone ring that she wore on her left hand. Her father asked if it was an engagement ring. His daughter replied, "Dad, it's my love ring."

The couple spent a couple of family evenings at the Gillian's, but as the New Year approached as well as Phil's trip to Turkey, the two celebrated alone. It was a special time for the two to be together, to hold each other, and make love. And too, Phil was able to tell MaryRose a great deal of what she could expect overseas. Phil left on the third and two days later MaryRose was on the plane to China.

An FBI agent who introduced himself as John Carter met her at the airport in China. He drove to the field office where MaryRose received her papers and official documents. She sat down with the director and he informed her of where and what her job was to investigate. He gave her keys to the apartment complex where she would be staying. It didn't take long for the office to be very impressed with their new field agent.

John Carter drove her to the new residence and gave her a cell phone for her use in China and said, "If you need anything or I can help you in any way, take my card with my cell number and don't ever hesitated to use it. The lab you will be working in is just around the corner, making it easy for you to get to; however, any time you need a car, here is the number to call and just show them your ID and it will be charged to the field office," he said as he handed the information needed to her. She thanked him and indeed promised him she would no doubt be calling him.

MaryRose was pleased with the apartment; it was clean and certainly adequate for her needs. She put her clothes away and laid all her credentials and information out on the small desk provided. She sat down and poured over all the information given to her, which she quickly memorized. It was nearing the dinner hour, so she decided to do a little exploring of the neighborhood, plus take a look at the building where she would be working. Her knowledge of the Chinese language was practically nil, only knowing a few words. She would pick up a translation book as soon as she found one. Mair walked for blocks around her apartment building and found some grocers, restaurants, and shops. The lab and offices where she would be working were in a six-story modern looking building. It was dusk and she decided to grab a bite to eat.

MaryRose arrived at her workplace at eight forty-five the next morning. She was told her laboratory where she was to work was on the fifth floor. She knocked on the door, which looked like a reception area. The Chinese woman sitting behind the desk was wearing a white lab coat so MaryRose wasn't sure if she was the receptionist, but greeted her in Chinese, "Nihoa." The woman smiled and said, "good morning, how can I help you?" MaryRose gave her the credentials the field office gave her. She was going to be doing investigative work, but undercover, and certainly not as an FBI agent.

"Yes, Miss Gillian, we've been expecting you; in fact we've been very anxious awaiting your arrival. Your offices are located on the fifth floor. Take the elevator and turn left and your offices are at the end of the hallway, number 525 and 526. Once MaryRose was in the room 525, there was a Chinese gentleman working diligently over the microscopes. A woman appeared from what seemed out of nowhere, introduced herself as AhKum, and escorted MaryRose to another lab. She introduced a Chinese woman, Chou and a Caucasian man, Carl, also a Chinese man by the name of Samuel; a strange threesome. They were all scientists working on the project MaryRose was investigating. She was about to know them well.

As the weeks passed, her work was more individual, but at least once or twice a day she worked side-by-side with each of them. It became apparent to MaryRose after being there a couple of weeks that they were couple of numbers off in their calculations. Even one number off would mean disaster. She had to memorize whatever she saw missing. It would be too dangerous to take any paperwork regarding the project out of the lab. She got to know Chou and Karl pretty well, but Samuel was a mystery. He seldom spoke, and when he did, it was always in Chinese. For some reason, MaryRose thought he might be the missing link in the project. She couldn't put her finger on yet what it was. One evening leaving work, she and Karl went down the elevator together and he asked her to have dinner with him. She accepted and he drove her to an American restaurant on the other side of the city. MaryRose found it interesting and as the evening wore on, she found Karl more interesting. He pretty much told her his life story, but what interested Mair more was his relationship with Samuel. It turned out they had been friends for many years. So why didn't they talk to one another in or out of the lab? She purposely did not want to delve into their past and was pretty sure they weren't a gay couple.

Once back in her apartment, Mair got out the direct line cell phone to John. She related the missing numbers she memorized of the day's work in the lab. She also asked him to look into both Karl's and Samuel's backgrounds. "Something's not right and I just can't put my finger on it. See what you can find out."

"Please remember you're dealing with some bad characters and don't leave anything in writing anywhere. We think your apartment is being watched but I assure you we are watching the watchers. Take good care, and I'll talk to you tomorrow night. Start using this second code then."

Near the end of Mair's second month in China, she went out to lunch. This was unusual because her so-called colleagues always had lunch brought in. AhKum didn't come in this particular day and it was she who always brought the lunch. Mair volunteered and as she was bringing lunch back into the building, she did a double take because she swore she saw her Notre Dame short time roommate, Myling. She immediately went back out, but the woman she saw was nowhere in sight. The next day Mair, faked feeling ill and said she needed air. It was about the same time she brought lunch in the day before. This time she stood outside where she could watch people coming out and sure enough within minutes, MyLing was exiting the building. MaryRose walked right up to her and said, "MyLing, fancy meeting you here in China." The look on MyLing's face was that of shock

"How come MaryRose you don't look any older than you did at Notre Dame and what the hell are you doing here?"

"I came to see you, and waited for you to come back to the states and go to Harvard with me and you never showed. How come? What's new with you? What are you doing?" MaryRose's instincts told her this woman wasn't glad to see her. Within the next minute or two, MyLing said she was in a rush because she had a meeting. She was quickly out of sight. MaryRose went back into her building to go back to the lab. She waited by the door and sure enough MyLing came back and was entering the building in a hurry. MaryRose quickly left the building and was out of sight of the doors. She peeked around just as MyLing entered an elevator. MaryRose rushed back inside and watched MyLing's elevator rise and stop at the fifth floor – same floor as the lab was on. Mair waited a few minutes and walked up the stairs to the fifth floor. As far as she could see no one saw her enter the stairwell. When she reached the fifth floor, she casually sauntered out into the hallway. Mair had no idea exactly where the stairs exited in relation to the lab. Fortunately, it was right around the corner, which she quickly entered.

That night when she got to her apartment, she knew things were getting very tight and dangerous. John's cell phone was blinking, warning her not to pick up the phone until it was no longer blinking. John had told her the apartment was under surveillance, so Mair went around checking the booby traps she had planted in order to tell if anyone was here. Before she was done, John's blinking stopped so she immediately put a call in to him. And as soon as he picked up the call, he said. "Code purple." And the phone went dead. Mair knew not to get in touch with him; he would one way or the other get in touch with her probably within the hour. Forty-five minutes later, there was a knock on her door, but when she opened it, no one was there. However, there was a piece of paper that had been slipped under the door. She quickly picked it up, read it, and burned it immediately. The note told her that within the next few weeks, she will have solved the problem, and to hang in there. There would be an FBI agent in the vacant apartment next door to her and if for any reason, she should tap three times in quick succession on the wall.

MaryRose went to work the next day and everything seemed normal, if there was a normal, but it didn't appear anything was different. She continued to gather the needed information and relay it to John. As long as she was there, she never saw Myling again. By the end of her third month, John told her to be ready to leave China in two weeks' time and to continue to be vigilant. Things seemed to go smoothly in the lab, as a matter of fact, there were no more missed numbers to memorize, which Mair felt was a good indication - problem solved.

MaryRose's felt her last two weeks would be easy with no complications. However, the very first day as she was walking to work, John's cell beeped liked she had never heard before. At first, she thought it might be in need of a new battery, but knew she didn't dare take it out of her sleeve pocket on a public street. She knew a few stores down was a café. She went in to order a cup of coffee, and while waiting went to the restroom. She nonchalantly scanned the Café's customers. When she knew she was the only one in the restroom. She took out John's cell and called him. "Thank God MaryRose. I thought I'd never get you. I see you haven't entered your building, and that's good."

"What is going on?" Mair whispered, and in a whispered voice continued, "I'm in café Henhao picking up a cup of coffee. I have put the earpiece in my ear and I have left the restroom and I'm headed to the counter to pick up my coffee. I can't speak.

"Okay, I have it spotted. A man in a white windbreaker has followed you since you left the apartment. He is now leaning outside against the Café window. Do you see him - beep once, if you do. Okay, walk out the door and walk across the street - see the man wearing a baseball cap." Mair beeped once again. "You're almost up to him, act like you are old friends. The packet he is handing you, take it- good, continue to your office walking fast. An agent wearing a navy jacket will follow you into the elevator making sure there is no one else in the elevator. He will give you further instructions." John's signal went dead.

All happened exactly as John said it would. The agent said. "They're suspicious it might be you who found their code. Go into the lab and do what you ordinarily would do. Remember, they will closely watch every move you make, as we closely watch you. He gave her a transmitter to wear inside her bra. I will be in the lab next door and you will be constantly monitored. Mair entered her lab and said good morning. Chou, Karl, and Samuel were busy at their tables. Only Karl looked up and asked if she was okay, since she was late.

"Yes I know, and I'm sorry, just couldn't wake up this morning. I had a quick breakfast and a cup of coffee and left the apartment. I really was having a hard time waking up, so I thought another cup of coffee might help and I stopped at the Café." Karl nodded. There was something strange; he kept turning his head back and forth to the left. At first, Mair didn't see why but suddenly the man in the white windbreaker was standing next to Chou. He moved from each lab station to the next, spending quite a bit of time at Samuels. He moved on to my station. I turned and looked at him and introduced myself and asked him his name. He didn't answer, and I immediately scratched my chest while he motioned me into another room.

"Sit down," he demanded as he pointed to a chair. "Where do you come from?"

"America."

"Don't be smart with me - America big country – where?"

"The little town named Georgetown across the Potomac River from Virginia." It was obvious he had no idea where Georgetown was."

"Near what big city?"

"Oh, Arlington. Why do you ask?"

"You lie."

"Why would I lie – I don't understand. You asked where I came from and I told you."

The man bent down and went eyeball to eyeball with MaryRose, "You think I don't know, you smart ass

American" and with that he gave her a tremendous forceful slap across her face, which knocked her to the floor. Immediately he heard the front door open and yelled, "Who there." Almost before he got the words out of his mouth, there were six FBI Agents with Rifles drawn and the agents were putting restraints on Mr. Chwousaki. One agent helped MaryRose to her feet and guided her out the door to the elevator. John's cell phone was buzzing like crazy.

"You better answer. Or John will have a whole squad over here." She did, and assured John she was okay. "Tell Tim to bring you right over here. You needn't go to your apartment; all your belongings have been brought here already."

They arrived at the field office minutes later and when John saw MaryRose he said, "My Lord MaryRose you did get socked. Maybe we should get you to a doctor, the whole side of your face is black and blue, and it's probably going to swell."

"I really don't think it's necessary, but I'd love to lie down for a while."

"No problem. Tim take her over to the Ritz, I'll make the arrangements. I'll call you later. MaryRose, how about a really good dinner. But truthfully, I want to get you out of China early tomorrow morning. Okay?

At eight a.m. MaryRose boarded a Delta airline along with Tim. "Are you flying with me?" She asked

"You bet I have to deliver this precious cargo because my friend Phil needs you home."

CHAPTER SEVENTEEN

As her Delta plane prepared to land at Reagan International Airport, MaryRose's anxiety was at a high pitch. It has been almost four months since she seen or heard from Phil and now she would be in his arms within minutes. Once the plane landed all passengers were directed to customs. "Gee Tim, I have nothing to declare. Maybe I do, assuming John had my luggage put on this plane."

"Don't worry, MaryRose. Once we get to the custom clerk just show your badge. They won't even ask to see your briefcase. Once they see your badge, they'll direct you to where your luggage is located." This is exactly what happened; she was directed to a room number, which is located right outside of customs. Also Phil was standing right outside of customs. Phil and MaryRose's union was a site to see. Poor Tim didn't know where to look. Eventually the three of them got to the cabstand. Tim told them to go in the first available and he would follow in the next cab. Both MaryRose and Tim had to report in at the Bureau and hand in their report to Brad before going on furlough or to their next assignment.

The poor cabdriver driving Phil and MaryRose had a difficult time keeping his eye on the road when the action in the back seat was far more interesting. When they reached the FBI building downtown DC, the loving couple waited for Tim to arrive before entering the building. Rush hour in DC is ridiculous but eventually Tim's cab pulled to the curb.

The three entered Brad's office to the cheers of the office staff in particular Clara, who obviously was happy to see MaryRose – but concerned when she saw her bruised face. Even conservative Brad gave her a hug. After the greetings, Brad ushered MaryRose into his office with her briefcase for the debriefing even though he was aware of most of the happenings in China through John's office. However, it was important he get MaryRose's opinion and reactions to the problems she faced. Brad was visibly upset about her facial bruises and wanted to know exactly what happened. When all the reporting was finished, Brad said, "I am proud of you, MaryRose, you did a fantastic job, and your abilities were certainly noted. It's good to have you back and I wouldn't hesitate to depend on your capabilities for any job that comes up. But for now, both you and Phil will have the next ten days free." That statement brought a broad smile to MaryRose's face.

Phil and Mair went to their favorite restaurant in Georgetown. Mair realized it was the best food she had in months. It was dark by the time they reached Mair's apartment at the Murphys, but as soon as Phil's car pulled into the driveway, the Murphys back outside light went on. They didn't expect anybody in their driveway. Mr. Murphy came out of his house and halfway down the steps of his porch, he saw Phil get out of the car and went to the passenger side door to open it for MaryRose. "Oh my," he yelled to Mrs. Murphy, "it's our tenants, MaryRose and Phil." MaryRose gave Mr. Murphy a big hug and said she was glad to be home. "We are glad to see you and know you two are safe. We'll let you get settled and talk tomorrow."

By the time the two got in the apartment, neither one could keep their hands off of each other. They didn't bother to turn on any lights until they got into the bedroom. They stripped each other and made love.

The next morning, (actually it was almost noon) not having anything in the apartment to eat, Phil ran down to the market and brought back breakfast food. It was really the first time Phil had a chance to talk to her about China. His concern was the fact she was hurt. Other than that, he knew better than to ask any questions. Mair called her parents and made plans for a family dinner the following night. The couple spent this leisure time, with family and friends. Phil bought a small grill and invited the Murphys for a barbecue. They rented canoes to race each other on the Potomac; they took long walks and generally did what they wanted when they wanted and if they wanted. On the seventh day, Phil got a call that in two days, he would be leaving and on the eighth day, MaryRose got her call back to duty.

This is how the two FBI agents lived for the next six years. They both loved their jobs and really would have it no other way. Plus Brad tried very hard to work it out, so every six months or so these two people in love had the opportunity to be with each other. Sometimes it might be just for a couple of days and other times a couple of weeks. After each separation, their love for each other was stronger than before.

After the fifth year in FBI service, different parts of the world became very tense and Phil worried if something should happen to him. He wanted Mair to be taken care of and thought they should get married. However, Mair pointed out, if something happened to either one of them, each had their own benefits.

"Is that the real reason Mair, or is the reason you just don't want to be married?"

"Would it be possible for me to love you anymore, married or not? Phil, we have such a good life together. We've both seen married agents at different times, and I haven't met one couple that is still married. I don't know why. I've always thought marriage brought two people closer together. It seems in our business it doesn't work. Neither one of us will ever be in need financially. I want to keep on loving you for the rest of my life, and there isn't a doubt in my mind it could possibly be any different." So they continued as things were, and their life was very happy. Everyone certainly considered them a couple. Some years had passed before MaryRose's mom asked one afternoon when the two were out for lunch together if there were any plans for a baby. Actually, Mair was surprised the subject had not been brought up before. Her daughter answered, "It isn't that Phil, and I haven't thought about having a baby, but Mom being an international special agent it would be almost impossible to be good parents. I know you worked since you were married, but at least you could come home at night, and there would be weekends to enjoy your children. I for one never felt neglected. The life today in foreign countries can be dangerous and no place to bring up children."

"I can understand your concern and I think you're right. Don't misunderstand but a baby from you would make us overjoyed. Speaking of babies your brother is expecting their third."

"Really, that's exciting. Do they know what sex it's going to be - what they have a little girl and boy now, right?"

"Yes, Chuck and Chris are great parents, and if they know the sex of this baby they're keeping it a secret," her Mom commented

"I'm sure they take after you and Dad. What about Lyn, does she have a steady beau these days?

"Like you, she's one popular gal, but I think right now she's interested in finishing college. You know she wants to be a doctor, didn't you?"

"She mentioned that the last time I saw her. You and Dad have to be proud bringing up two lawyers and a doctor. That really is something to talk about. You know Mom when I think about it, how lucky we've been, not only having outstanding parents, but there was always Mattie and Lyn has always had Gracie to lean on."

"Yes my dear, we have been fortunate and Dad and I are as proud as we can be of each and every one of you. And I might add, we all are very fond of Phil. He truly is one nice young man and if you ever do choose to marry, your Dad would be elated."

That evening at dinner at the Gillian household, Bill was interested to know all about Marianne's lunch with Mair. "Bill, it was so good to see her, and she is happy as can be. We talked about her having children and afterwards I understood her position on the subject."

"Are they planning on marriage, first of all?"

"I don't think so as long as they both are federal agents."

"What's that to do with anything?" Marianne told him about their conversation about bringing children into the world as long as they were international agents. Bill listened carefully and understood his daughter's position, but still was disappointed.

Right after the mother-daughter lunch together, MaryRose was sent to Africa and Phil had already arrived in the Middle East. Every time the two were in any foreign country, Bill Gillian worried. But this was the life they chose and for all intents purpose; it was what they wanted and enjoyed doing.

Phil came stateside two months later, but was sent to another trouble area in the Middle East four days later. He was still there when MaryRose came home. While she was in Brad's office debriefing her assignment in Africa, Brad buzzed Clara to put in the call. Several minutes later Clara said the call came through. Brad picked up the receiver said "hi" and handed the phone to MaryRose. She almost fainted when she heard Phil's voice. The conversation wasn't very long because he was in a war zone and the reception was poor, but she did hear how much he loved her and wanted her to tell Brad to get him the hell home. After that, the reception failed completely. Mair immediately relayed Phil's request and asked, "Brad will Phil be home soon?"

"MaryRose before you arrived stateside this morning I looked up Phil's schedule and he is due back in three weeks. I doubt there is any way I can make it sooner. I will keep on it though."

Brad didn't mention he was worried. Phil was in a difficult place where the fighting was fierce and just getting to our airbase was a chancy situation. Getting through to Brad's contacts presently was next to impossible; however, he could still reach the airfield. For the rest of the day and into the night he kept trying to get through to any one of the operatives who were anywhere near the fighting zone. For most of the time, he had limited success. Clara found him asleep in the chair when she got to work the next morning. She immediately brewed some coffee and true to form, the smell of brewing coffee awakened Brad.

"Oh Clara what time is it – are there any transmissions coming through?"

"It looks like several arrived about an hour ago and…."Clara didn't finish but she ripped of the paper from the machine and with tears in her eyes handed it to Brad. He quickly read it and shouted, "Damn, damn," and his entire body went weak as he slumped down putting his hands over his eyes. Clara quietly walked out of his office. She knew it was time for him to be alone. Shortly after, he opened his office door, came into the outer office carrying yet another communique, and handed it to Clara.

"Brad, there is still hope."

"I pray you're right," Brad hesitated a moment, "Call MaryRose and asked her to come to the office at her earliest convenience. She'll probably ask why, just say I have some information about Phil. Make it short and sweet so you don't have to go into any detail. I'm going in to take a quick shower now; put any important call on hold and alert me by a knock on the door."

"No problem." Clara said as she watched Brad walk away a broken man. She went to her desk, made the call, and lied to MaryRose, telling her she had no idea why Brad wanted to see her. Clara knowing MaryRose was so intuitive and would arrive in a short time; she went into Brad's office and straightened out the paperwork. In other words, made things look at normal as possible.

It must have been minutes when the outer office door opened and MaryRose called "Is anybody home?" Clara came out of Brad's office and said,

"Wow, you made it over here in record time. Brad's waiting for you. Go right into his office." Clara's heart sank knowing what Brad had to tell her. At one point, she overheard MaryRose's crying, "No, no, dear Lord. Help him." Her heart went out to both MaryRose and Brad - having to talk about the person they both sincerely loved. It was some time before Brad's office door opened, and Brad and MaryRose walked out. Brad told Clara he'd be out of the office to take MaryRose to the airport.

MaryRose walked over to Clara and said, "I have to go, Clara. I have to see Phil and as long as there is a chance he's alive I have to take that chance – I have to." Clara hugged her and said.

"I know and I'll pray for both of you," and as she let her go added, "God bless you both."

As soon as they arrived at the airport, they went directly to the FBI office where they picked up MaryRose's ticket, temporary passport, currency for both US and

German markets. In the meantime, Brad went to the wires to get the latest information concerning Phil. He breathed a sigh of relief, because he was able to tell MaryRose everything was status quo. They had over an hour before her flight was due to leave, so Brad suggested they grab a bite to eat. MaryRose asked Brad to call her parents and the Murphys to tell them where she was and why. It was difficult for the two of them to make small talk; MaryRose's mind was consumed with thoughts of Phil, as was Brad's.

Finally, it was time to board the plane and Brad double checked MaryRose to be sure she had everything she needed and promised to make the telephone calls she wanted right away. He put his arms around her and said, "You are a strong woman and I know you'll bring peace to Phil. As soon as he sees you he'll be better." He took her by the arm and escorted her to the plane promising her he would be in constant touch and if she needed anything, all she had to do was call.

With tears streaming down her cheeks, she managed a smile and said, "I know why Phil considers you such a good friend. Thank you for everything."

As soon as the plane was in the sky, he went back to the FBI office in the airport and called Clara. "The plane just took off and I want to call her parents. You have their phone number and also her landlords, Mr. Murphy's phone number. Please get them for me, I'll wait." Clara returned and gave Brad the numbers he wanted also reminded him that both Mr. and Mrs. Gillian would no doubt be at work. Did he want their work numbers also? "You're right Clara," he hesitated for a moment and then said, "You know, Clara, I think I'll go right over to Mr. Gillian's office. I'd rather talk to them face-to-face, if I can."

Brad left the airport, went directly to Gillian's law office, and told his secretary, he would like to see Mr. Gillian. She asked who was calling, and as soon as she saw his badge, picked up her phone and said, "Mister Gillian, there's a Mr. Brad Hampton, an FBI agent here to see you." She hung up the phone and told Mr. Hampton to go right in. Actually, Mr. Gillian opened his office door before Brad had the chance. They shook hands and entered the office

"It would be unusual for an FBI agent to come knocking on my door, if it wasn't to tell me something about my daughter FBI agent, MaryRose Gillian."

"Mr. Gillian your daughter is fine. I'm here at her request to tell you she is on an airplane to Germany. Phil Kern is in a German hospital in critical condition after being wounded in Pakistan. I requested your daughter come to my office this morning to give her the news. There wasn't a doubt in her mind, she must go there and be with Phil. She is in flight now, due to arrive at seven in the evening our time."

It was obvious hearing this news upset her father and he asked if there was any way he could talk to her. Brad told him he could try her cell phone but there has been problems getting calls through to the hospital. "At this point I'm not sure where she'll be staying, but I will be informed of her arrival and where she might be staying. However, knowing your daughter I don't think she'll leave the hospital."

"You do know my daughter," Mr. Gillian said and added, "I sincerely appreciate you coming here and if possible, I'd like to request your office keep us informed. Phil Kern has become a very important part of our lives and all the Gillians truly care." The two men shook hands as Bill Gillian thanked Brad again. Once back at the office, Brad made the call to the Murphys who was equally shocked to hear the news. "Mr. Murphy, Miss Gillian left in such a hurry, she asked me to call you for you to please check her doors. She left in such a hurry, she isn't sure if she locked them." Her landlord said of course he would and went on to say, what a fine young man Phil is and he and the Mrs. would be praying for him and his darling, MaryRose. "They are such a fine young couple, so considerate. Thank you, sir, for calling."

Brad waited at the office until he was sure MaryRose's plane had landed in Germany and she was in fact at the hospital. Being sure of that, he checked his contact to find out Phil's condition. When he received a communiqué answering his question, it read Phil's condition had gone from critical to grave, and Brad's heart sank. He immediately called his operative in the area and asked if agent Gillian had arrived. "Yes sir, she arrived about an hour ago. Agent Kern was aware she was here and said to anyone who could hear him she was the love of his life. He smiled and died several minutes later, holding her hand."

"Where is agent Gillian now?"

"I believe she is still here in the hospital administration room. And she's possibly trying to get in touch with you as we speak."

"I'll hang up now and if you see her please tell her I'll wait for her call at my office, no matter how late it is." Brad hung up the phone and paced back and forth, mostly in anger he no longer had his best friend and was impatient wanting to hear from MaryRose. About an hour later, her call finally came through. She was too upset to say much only that she was going to stay there and accompany Phil's body to the airport, and will stay with him on the flight back to Washington. She will call Brad as soon as the arrangements are made. Brad looked at his watch, it was only nine-fifteen at night, so decided to call the Gillian's house. Bill Gillian answered the phone after the first ring and Brad gave him the news. "As soon as I know the day and arrival time here in Washington, I will call you immediately. Your daughter is at the hospital right now, so you might not be able to get through to her. Keep trying and if you can't get her at the hospital, I know you will get her once she is outside of the hospital. Any further information, I will notify you right away.

"This is a terrible loss, Brad, as well as a tremendous loss for MaryRose. I suppose the loss goes well beyond us; from what I gather, he was one ace special agent for the FBI. Thank you for your concern." Brad made it a point to call the Murphys first thing the next morning. They too felt the loss and were very concerned for MaryRose.

Brad had arrived at the airport earlier than most to be sure all the arrangements he made were in place. Shortly after eight a.m. FBI special agents, all dressed in dark suits and ties, arrived in front of the hangar where the plane from Germany would dock. Not long after, every member of MaryRose's family started to arrive followed shortly by Mr. and Mrs. Murphy and other close neighbors. By the time, the plane landed there really was an unexpected large crowd. Brad and the pallbearers headed by the Gillian's parish priest walked out to the landed plane to escort the casket to the hangar. When everything was set in place, the pallbearers wheeled the casket to the stairs as MaryRose was descending from the plane. The procession headed by the priest, closely followed by Brad and MaryRose following the casket and the pallbearers at its side walked to the waiting hearse. As previously arranged, a line of funeral cars stopped at the hangar to pick up all the mourners and followed the hearse to Georgetown's Trinity Church where the funeral mass was celebrated. Brad gave the eulogy followed by one given by Bill Gillian. Both were heartwarming and emotional and celebrated Phil's life. There wasn't a dry eye in the church. MaryRose sat in the front pew in between her Father and Brad. One would wonder, although in body was she there in mind; she seemed almost paralyzed. When the mass was over the priest announced the burial would be at the cemetery next to the Gillian family church outside of Arlington, Virginia. All who wish to attend are most welcome and directions will be found in the rear of the church. A reception will follow the burial at the Gillian's home and directions also are at the rear of the church.

The following day the quiet in the Gillian household was almost deafening. It was like everyone was afraid to make noise for fear of disturbing MaryRose. About ten o'clock that morning, Mair came down to the kitchen, gave Gracie a hug, and thanked her for all she had done to make the reception a wonderful event. Gracie made her a great breakfast and brewed her special coffee, which Mair loved. As she sipped her coffee, she walked around the house and read each card attached to the many floral arrangements. She went back to the kitchen and said, "You know Gracie, we should take these flowers over to the nursing home. They are so beautiful and more people than us should enjoy them. Let's do this after breakfast. Okay?" Mair's father overheard this conversation as he stood in the hallway. He smiled because in his heart he knew his daughter would survive her loss and will continue to make other people happy.

CHAPTER EIGHTEEN

MaryRose stayed at her parent's house for about a week after the funeral. She took long walks and visited Christine and her nephews and niece. She talked to Auntie Marge and promised she would come see her in the not-too-distant future. She went to the high school soccer field and watched Charlyn play who is now a on the senior varsity team, and also it's Captain. The team loved to see Lyn's big sister come to some of their practices. MaryRose's reputation was well known at the school and some of the hallways sported pictures of MaryRose in action.

A week after Phil's funeral, Mair and her parents were sitting in the sun porch having their after dinner coffee. It was then she announced she would be going back to her apartment in DC.

"Are you thinking of what's coming next Mair?" Her Dad asked.

"I'm really not sure Dad what comes next, but yes, I've done a lot of thinking, but haven't decided on anything definite at this point. I'm positive though, it's time to get on with my life. One of the first things I plan on doing is to talk to Brad. I'm sure I'm not the first widow he's given advice."

"Sounds like a good plan to me," her Mother commented. The next morning, after Lyn was off to school and her Mom and Dad to work, Mair sat down in the kitchen with Gracie to have breakfast together. "Your Mom told me last night you're going back to the apartment today, so I packed up a little welcome home basket to get you started refilling the empty cupboards." With that, Gracie brought out a huge picnic basket from the pantry.

"Gracie, you are so thoughtful and I love you. I'm truly happy Mom, Dad and Lyn found you to be part of our family. You certainly are the answers to our prayers."

Mair drove into the Murphy's driveway about two o'clock that afternoon. It is a beautiful fall day, so she was surprised not to see the Murphys sitting on their front porch rockers, but then she noticed the car was not in the garage either. It took several trips from her car to the apartment to get all her belongings in the house. She was carrying her last load when the Murphys drove up the driveway. They were excited to see her and there were hugs and kisses all around.

Every inch of the apartment was a reminder of Phil. Her first night back was much harder than she imagined and she cried herself to sleep. Mair spent the next morning putting things where they belonged and trying to cope without Phil. She finally decided to call Brad who was overjoyed to hear from her. He wanted her to come downtown and have lunch with him. She declined and said, "How about I meet you tomorrow after work at Kelly's pub? I have so much to talk to you about."

"Sounds like a good plan. Can you meet me there about five-thirty?"

"I look forward to seeing you – see you tomorrow." As soon as she hung the phone up, she dialed the Sisters of the Angels convent and asked to speak to Mother Mary Margaret.

"MaryRose how wonderful to hear from you, tell me how you are, – tell me everything," Auntie Marge said.

"I'm doing fine. After all I'm on God's side of the tracks – as my Sister Mary Margaret would say." And they both laughed.

"You will come see me soon, I hope."

"That's exactly why I'm calling. When is a good time for you? Is this weekend good for you and do you have an empty bed to spare?"

"Absolutely."

"Great I'll be up Saturday afternoon around two o'clock. Can't wait to see you, you're exactly what the Doctor ordered." MaryRose smiled when she hung up and knew Auntie Marge is just what she needed.

Sitting in her living room where she and Phil sat many times making plans for their future together and now she is sitting alone trying to make plans just for her. Dear God, how quickly life changes – help me survive without Phil – let me follow your guiding light – let me see it. Mair sat there and her mind was like a Rolodex – many thoughts – one after the other rolled through her mind. She looked at the clock and it was almost five o'clock. She couldn't believe she had been on the couch that long. She jumped up and got ready to meet Brad.

As Mair walked into Kelly's she immediately spotted Brad sitting at the bar as the light from the open door streamed in the darkened bar, Brad immediately turned and saw Mair, walking towards him. He stood and guided her to a booth. Once seated across the table from each other, he reached across and took Mair's hands, "Mair, it's good to see you – you look great. Tell me how are things going for you?"

"I'm okay, Brad. It's like each new day Phil gets farther and farther away, but I'm desperately trying to hold on to him. I remember when, Mattie died; I don't know if you knew her, but with Mom and Dad working Mattie really brought me up. She wasn't a housekeeper, rather a friend to all of us and an important part of our family. When she died a number of years ago, I kept on holding onto to her for weeks. I just couldn't let – let her go."

"But Mair in time you did let Mattie go but you never forgot her and you'll never stop loving her. In time, this will be the same for Phil, and you have to allow yourself the time."

"Brad, you always have the right words – thank you." The two friends continued to talk and Brad at one point, turned the conversation to the FBI. He told Mair of different projects going on now and it was obvious hearing about the FBI sparked her interest.

"How about it Mair, if I put you on a sabbatical leave for a year or two it could be sooner could be later? That's immaterial at this point. You are an amazing agent and I think you loved what you were doing."

"I do love it Brad and I think in the back of my mind I would love to come back."

"Great – you're living in the same apartment with the same phone number right."

"Yes, and you have my cell phone number. I will always be sure you know where I am and how to get in touch with me." Mair assured him.

Brad took her hands again and said, "MaryRose you know full well I'm always here for you and if you need anything, any time, please call on me. It's bad enough we lost Phil. I don't want to lose you."

A few days after her visit with Brad, she called her Auntie Marge and asked if she could come to the convent for a few days. Her request was welcomed with a great deal of joy.

That Saturday Mair arrived at the convent and faithful Sister Joel opened the garden gate for her. "Sister Joel, it is so good to see you," MaryRose said as she gave the nun a hug.

"Your Aunt could hardly contain herself waiting for your arrival. Come, she is waiting in her office."

"Sister Joel, how is the Mother Superior?" My mother says she is slowing down a bit these days."

As they approached Mother Mary Margaret, there she was waiting at the door with her wonderful smile. Mair didn't realize Sister Joel left and came back shortly with a tray of tea and goodies.

"You know Sister Joel, ever since I was a young woman, and probably long before, it always amazed me how you – and the other sisters – walk around without a sound. Not only do you not make any noise, but you walk like you're floating on air. That must be part of the training. I bet you're not allowed to receive the final vows if you're heard walking," MaryRose kidded.

Auntie Marge and Mair talked about the family and her thrill seeing Chuck's beautiful family and how Lyn was following in MaryRose's footsteps. Finally, she approached the subject of Phil. "You know my dear how fond I was of Phil. He was a delightful, sincere person. I know his death is a terrible loss for you. I pray for you both every day. Phil is with God and at peace. You will find his peace by just asking for it. Stay close to your faith my dear, and you too will find the comfort you need."

"Auntie Marge, God's words coming from you gives me a lot of comfort." They walked in the garden together before the evening meal while Mair expressed her desire to face the future. MaryRose joined all the nuns at dinner. There were two long tables and MaryRose estimated there were sixteen sisters waiting to take their final vows and four novices who have yet to take their initial vows. She glanced at the four young ones, and oh yes, they were young. Mair hoped they would accept the Mother Superior's advice.

After the meal was over the evening, Vespers were sung. MaryRose closed her eyes and listen to the beautiful voices; she was amazed at the peace that came over her. She and her Aunt visited for a short while before retiring for the night.

Mair slept in the small cubicle as all the nuns did. She had forgotten how small they really were, but then you don't need anything more. Early the next morning the Sisters routine started all over again. They all spent a great deal of time studying and going to classes, learning the reasons for their vocation and what their vocations meant to them. Auntie Marge allowed her to sit in any class she chose to. MaryRose was impressed with their dedication to learning and exploring their vocation.

Sunday evening Auntie Marge and MaryRose enjoyed some spare time together walking through the garden in the dim light of the autumn evening. MaryRose turned to her Aunt and said, "Auntie Marge, let's sit on this garden bench. I have so much I want to talk to you about."

"What is it my dear, your voice has such urgency in it?"

"Does it? Probably because in the back of my mind, I've wanted to ask you so many questions but never was sure if it was appropriate. Being with you the last couple of days, I realize that any question I have you will answer. God has given you the gift and you use it to counsel others."

"In a short time, the lights in the garden will go out. Let's you and I go into my room, where we can have a private conversation." The two women got up and hand in hand walked to Sister Mary Margaret's private room. "Now, MaryRose tell me what's on your mind; ask me anything."

"You know, we've talked before and how many times have I said I wanted to devote my life to God – I wanted to do God's work and I would go off and do anything but not God's work. Instead, I worked for my own pleasure. I worked at what I wanted to do—what I had been taught to do. I fell in love and I lived with Phil in what the church calls a sin, but in all honesty, I never considered I was living in sin. Do you believe that – do you believe after all my religious training and my desire to obey God I chose not to follow his commands? I've thought about this many, many times, and to be truthful, I don't understand why." MaryRose paused for a good minute or two while her Auntie Marge said nothing.

"I don't understand now why I want to take my final vows and devote my life only to God. I don't understand in my heart of hearts why I want desperately to become a nun, and yet want an outside life apart from the convent too. An outside life to investigate and explore the right and wrongs of this world that could help the weak solve problems, and perhaps educate the lesser of us." MaryRose hung her head down and prayed for an answer. Her Aunt got up from her chair, sat close to MaryRose on the couch, and held her hand tightly.

"My dear sweet child, some of the things you want answered will only be answered by God. There are many of us who felt over the years you have a vocation. Not the kind of vocation I had or of the women even forty or fifty years ago. I guess the best way to put it is other than the cloistered nuns, convent life has changed and probably for the better. Yes, I'm happy with the changes. The nun of today can follow a career within the limits of the church. You know yourself, nuns can walk down a street and look just like any other woman; in fact, and you can't identify them as a nun at all. Therefore, what you're asking is certainly is in the realm of possibility. Remembering there will be some constrictions asked of you." MaryRose got up from the couch and went to the window overlooking the garden. She turned and walked over to her Aunt and knelt down in front of her and said -

"From what you say, Auntie Marge, there are possibilities for me."

"Yes, there are MaryRose. I want you to go back to your apartment and think hard about exactly what you want. Think of the things you want to do. Then figure out what you can do and what you can't do within the realm of reality. Think of our talk here this evening and then wrestle with your thoughts. Then come back here and we'll learn your answers."

The next morning, MaryRose left the convent and drove directly to her apartment in DC. The first thing she did in the apartment was to open all the windows, let sadness out, and the freshness of the air in. After she had a bite to eat, she sat at her desk and started to make a list of all the things she hoped for in her future; besides each listing she put how this could be accomplished. The second list, she wrote the things she did not want in her life; beside that list was one word. Why?

She stopped midafternoon and heated up a can of soup, and went right back to her lists. Mair read and reread her lists several times, wrote and rewrote several times too. As darkness fell and the chill entered her room, Mair put her lists aside and closed the windows. She put on a sweater, went outside, and took a long walk. Her mind was filled with the written lists. Before leaving the house, she had shortened the lists by crossing off the things that truly were meaningless, meaningless in the sense they might have been something she wanted, but after reasoning they really weren't important and would not accomplish an end result. She thought about what she had written plus what she crossed out and finally knew what to do. As she came to the conclusion, the gait of her walking became faster. She felt alive, confident, and sure of herself.

When Mair got back to her apartment, she immediately went over to her desk, picked up the mass of papers, and sorted them out. She came to the final page, looked at it again, and smiled. She put that page aside and tore up the others discarding them in the wastebasket, which gave her a tremendous sense of fulfillment.

First thing she did the next morning was to call Brad. He wasn't in yet so she asked Clara if he had any free time on his calendar to see her today. "I know he has an appointment this morning and isn't expected in the office – let me see here – MaryRose he should be able to see you about one-thirty this afternoon. If there's a change, I'll call you right away on your cell."

In the meantime, she washed out a few things before she raided Gracie's picnic basket and made herself a wonderful sandwich. Before she knew it, it was time to leave for downtown DC. As she walked into the FBI headquarters, a wonderful feeling came over MaryRose of self-confidence. "Brad is waiting for you in the office – go right in." Clara smiled.

After the greetings were over, MaryRose said, "Brad, I'm going to take you up on a sabbatical and it probably will be close to two years." Brad started to speak but MaryRose said she felt he deserved it explanation. "Brad, I want you to hear me out because what I have to tell you is well—a little unusual; you might say extremely unusual."

"I assure you MaryRose you have my full attention and curiosity."

"Brad, I'm going upstate Virginia to the Sisters of the Angels convent. There I will be studying to become a nun." MaryRose saw the expression of disbelief on Brad's face and quickly continued, "Before I go any further Brad, the nun of today is not the nun you and I pictured years ago. She is a modern woman who looks just like any woman you might see on the street. She dresses the same, with perhaps on her lapel or somewhere obvious a small cross. She works outside of the convent within the restrictions of the convent. Her life is dedicated to God instead of dedicated to herself."

"MaryRose you must admit this is a little out of the ordinary. What I mean is up to this moment I've never been faced by an FBI special agent who is a nun." Brad commented.

"I can believe that Brad, but ever since I was a young girl I've wanted to be a nun, and each time I was serious about it or thought I was serious about it, there was something else I thought I should do first. The biggest stumbling block was falling in love with Phil. Brad you know my credentials, and when you think about it, I've done it all. Now I do want to follow my vocation and if possible, still be an FBI agent."

"Actually, MaryRose, I have heard of the convent you're talking about. I believe you and Phil visited your Aunt Mother Superior at the convent" MaryRose nodded and Brad, continued, "I remember Phil was impressed with your Aunt and her surroundings."

"Yes he was. It really is amazing Brad, when you enter the convent garden gate, how the peace and serenity is overwhelming. Tomorrow I'm going to make an appointment to see the Mother Superior and tell her of my decision, and see if I can work out being a sister and a special agent at the same time. I would not have come to see you today if I thought it could not be worked out."

"Somehow MaryRose if anyone can work it out, I know you will."

La Maison Publishing, Inc.
www.lamaisonpublishing.com
ISBN: 978-0-9885902-7-4

CPSIA information can be obtained at www.ICGtesting.com
Printed in the USA
LVOW10s1941200114

370136LV00004B/7/P